ALBOM

Level 5

Retold by Nancy Taylor

ators: Andy Hopkins and Jocelyn Potter

Pearson Education Limited
Edinburgh Gate, Harlow,
Essex CM20 2JE, England
and Associated Companies throughout the world.

ISBN: 978-1-4082-6387-7

This edition first published by Pearson Education Ltd 2012

3 5 7 9 10 8 6 4

Original copyright © Mitch Albom, 2003
Text copyright © Pearson Education Ltd 2012
Illustrations by Jonathan Burton

Set in 11/14pt Bembo
Printed in China
SWTC/03

Published by Pearson Education Limited in association with
Penguin Books Ltd, and both companies being subsidiaries of Pearson PLC

Contents

Introduction

"God's greatest gift to you is the understanding of what happened in your life on Earth. Then you will find the peace you have been searching for."

This is a story that starts at the end of the main character's life on Earth. But after Eddie's death, the real story begins—in heaven. Most people have their own theories or beliefs about life after death, and when we read *The Five People You Meet in Heaven*, we can compare our own ideas with the situation that Eddie finds himself in. Do we think we will meet people in heaven after we die? Who might those people be? What will they say to us?

From the moment Eddie arrives in heaven, he begins to make sense of his life—and by association, we, the readers, make more sense of our own lives. We are taken on an exciting and emotional adventure of discovery. It is the most important journey that a person can make: a journey to understand the meaning of life.

Mitch Albom, an internationally famous and best-selling author, was born in 1958 in New Jersey, the second of three children. He has said that he was lucky to have wonderful, loving parents who encouraged him to try all kinds of things and to explore the world.

With this support, Mitch Albom showed a talent for different types of art from an early age, starting with drawing. But soon he switched to music and taught himself to play the piano. After graduating from college, he played in a band for several years, in Europe and in the United States. He also wrote and recorded several original songs. He always knew that he wanted to do something creative because he noticed that creative people were happier in their lives.

In his twenties, Mitch Albom decided to become a journalist and he began working, without pay, for the *Queens Tribune*. After further studies at Columbia University, he became a full-time journalist, working in New York, then Florida, and finally in Detroit, Michigan, where he moved in 1985. Detroit suited him and he found more openings for his many talents. He worked in newspapers, radio, and television, becoming the host of a popular daily talk show on radio and appearing regularly on a national TV sports channel.

In 1995, he married Janine Sabino. That same year he met Morrie Schwartz, one of his former college teachers, who was slowly dying of a terrible disease. Mitch Albom began visiting his old teacher regularly and decided to write a book based on their conversations. The purpose of writing *Tuesdays with Morrie* was to help pay the older man's medical bills, but it also moved Albom away from journalism into his new career as a writer of non-fiction books, novels, and plays.

Tuesdays with Morrie (1997) was on the New York Times best-seller list for four years. This success with a work of non-fiction led Mitch Albom to write another best-seller: *The Five People You Meet in Heaven* (2003), which sold more copies in hardback than any other first novel for adults in the United States. These books were followed by *For One More Day* (2006), which was chosen by Starbucks as the first book in their program to encourage more people to read, and then by *Have a Little Faith*, which was chosen by Oprah Winfrey as the best non-fiction book of 2009. The TV movie of *The Five People You Meet in Heaven* was watched by 19 million American viewers in 2004, making it the most popular TV movie of that year.

Mitch Albom has said that he gets his ideas for a book from the emotional moments in life—moments when he feels tears behind his eyes or when he finds it difficult to breathe. Then he asks himself what happened to push him to that point. He looks for something universal, something that all people feel. Then he knows he is looking at something important and, as he says, "I begin to create a story from that moment."

The moment that led to the creation of *The Five People You Meet in Heaven* was the death of the writer's Uncle Eddie, a man who always felt that his life didn't matter. Mitch Albom wanted to write a story in which a man like his Uncle Eddie arrives in heaven and learns that his life on Earth had meaning and importance.

The moment for *For One More Day* came from thinking about his mother's life. She always defended her son and his beliefs. By trying to imagine life without her, Mitch Albom knew that after his mother's death, he would want another day with her. That feeling gave him the background for the book.

His deep connection to his family and to people he cares about has led to another important concern in Mitch Albom's life. He has started four organizations which help disadvantaged people. The most recent of these, A Hole in the Roof, offers financial support to different religious groups; the groups are able to keep their buildings in good condition, so they can help homeless people in their neighborhoods. Mitch Albom also raises money for programs that help people improve their reading ability. You can read much more about his life and work at www.mitchalbom.com.

The Five People You Meet in Heaven deals with an experience that everyone will have one day: death. The book's tender, thoughtful, and human look at what might happen after death touches our hearts and dares us to think about our next life— but it also makes us consider how we are living today, here on Earth.

Like most of the other hours of his life, Eddie's last was spent at Ruby Park.

Chapter 1
The End

This is a story about a man named Eddie, and it begins at the end, with Eddie dying in the sun while he was at work at Ruby Park. It might seem strange to start a story at the end. But all endings are also beginnings. We just don't know it at the time.

♦

Like most of the other hours of his life, Eddie's last was spent at Ruby Park, a typical old-style American amusement park beside a great gray ocean. Visitors came to walk along the beach, to eat hot dogs and cotton candy, to win a prize at one of the shooting games, and, especially, to go on the rides. There were all the old-fashioned rides like the big Ferris wheels, the bumper cars, and the roller coasters, and there were some exciting new ones, too, like Freddy's Free Fall—and this was where Eddie's life would end.

At the time of his death Eddie was a short, broad, white-haired old man with a thick neck and strong arms. He used a cane and walked with a limp after being shot in the leg in World War II. Since then his left leg had caused him almost constant pain. His face was rough and lined after so many years in the sun, and his lower jaw stuck out, making him look prouder and less friendly than he really was. He kept a cigarette behind his left ear and a ring of keys hooked to his tool belt. He wore heavy shoes, an old cap, and a brown uniform. All of this suggested that he was a working man, and that was exactly what he was and had been for more than sixty years.

Eddie was the maintenance man at Ruby Park, which meant that he kept the rides running safely and smoothly. Every afternoon he walked through the park, checking each machine, looking for broken boards, loose screws, worn-out steel. And he was always listening. After all those years he could *hear* trouble and knew exactly how to fix the problem.

With fifty minutes left on Earth, Eddie took his last walk through Ruby Park. He was eighty-three today, but he didn't celebrate birthdays any more. Instead, he treated this day like a regular working day, and with forty minutes left to live, he went to the front of the line for the "Ghost," the biggest roller coaster in the park. Eddie went on every ride at least once a week, and the kids who knew him followed behind shouting, "Eddie!" "Take me, Eddie!" "Take me!"

Children liked Eddie. Not teenagers. Teenagers were trouble. They gave him headaches. They were always shouting, and throwing their trash on the ground. Children, on the other hand, were polite and nice. They liked Eddie and were attracted to him like cold hands to a fire. They played with his keys and begged to go on the rides with him. Today it would be the turn of two little brothers in baseball caps. "Here we go ... *Here we go!*" one of the boys shouted, and the other pulled Eddie's arm around his shoulder as they climbed into the ride.

Thirty-four minutes to live. The roller coaster came to a stop, and Eddie gave each boy a piece of candy before he walked slowly over to the maintenance building to cool down. He was following his regular, dull routine with no idea that his death was hardly more than half an hour away. And if he had known, what would he have done differently?

One of the maintenance crew, named Dominguez, was at the sink cleaning a wheel.

"Hey, Eddie," he said. "What's happening, man?"

"Same as usual, Dom," Eddie replied. "No problems yet today."

The workshop had a low ceiling and was dark and crowded with work tables and spare parts. Tools hung neatly on the walls—everything for maintaining the rides. Eddie had dreamed of leaving this job, of building a different kind of life. But the war came and his plans never worked out. Like his father before him, Eddie was the head of maintenance, or as the kids sometimes called him, "the ride man" at Ruby Park.

Thirty minutes left.

"Hey, happy birthday, I hear," Dominguez said. "Are you having a party?"

Eddie looked at him in disbelief. He thought how strange it was to be an old man working in an amusement park.

"Well, remember, I'm on vacation next week. Theresa and I are going to Mexico to see the family. And to have a big party! Have you ever been south of the border?" Dominguez asked.

"To Mexico?" Eddie said. "Kid, I've never been anywhere except where the army sent me."

Dominguez was quiet. Eddie thought for a moment and then took his wallet from his back pocket. He held out two twenty-dollar bills to Dominguez.

"Get your wife something nice," Eddie said.

Dominguez looked at the money and a big smile spread across his face. "Man! Are you sure?"

Eddie pushed the money into the young man's hand.

Twenty-six minutes to live. Eddie was walking along the boardwalk at the south end of Ruby Park. Business was slow. A long time ago, this park was *the* place to go in the summer. There had been big shows in the evenings—dance contests, fireworks, and even elephants. But very few people went to the old seaside amusement parks now; these days they went to the big new theme parks, where you paid $75 to get in and had your photograph taken with big furry movie characters. Ruby Park was a lot cheaper than those places, but it couldn't compete any more.

Eddie limped past the bumper cars and noticed a small

group of teenagers leaning over the metal gate at the exit of the ride. "Great," he thought. "Just what I need."

"Off," Eddie said, striking the gate with his cane. "Come on. It's not safe."

You could hear the sound of the electricity from the car poles that connected each bumper car to the ceiling.

The teenagers stared rudely at him.

"It's not safe," Eddie repeated. "Move along."

One of the teenagers, with a shaved head and a ring through his nose, laughed at Eddie, then climbed onto the gate and began shouting at the kids in the bumper cars.

"Come on, guys, drive over here and hit me!" he cried, waving his arms at the young drivers. "What are you afraid of?"

Eddie hit the metal gate so hard with his cane that he almost broke it. "MOVE!"

The teenagers quickly ran away.

One of the stories that went around about Eddie was about his days as a soldier. It was believed that he had fought in quite a few battles during the war. He'd been brave—even won a medal, they said. But toward the end of his time in the army, he got into a fight with one of his own men. According to the story, that's how Eddie was wounded. No one knew what happened to the other guy.

No one asked.

With nineteen minutes left on Earth, Eddie sat for the last time in his old wooden beach chair. His legs were red from the sun and the rest of his body showed signs of a hard life. His fingers were bent and stiff, after a lot of injuries from working on different machines. His nose had been broken several times in what he called "bar-room battles." He looked like a man who had been good-looking, but—like a boxer's—his face and body had taken a lot of punishment.

Now Eddie just looked tired. But when he had a few

minutes to sit and rest, he thought of the old days, when a band played in the evenings at Ruby Park, and people came to the Stardust Room to listen and to dance.

This was where Eddie had met Marguerite.

Every life has one true-love moment. For Eddie, it came on a warm September night after a thunderstorm, when the boardwalk was wet. Marguerite wore a yellow cotton dress and had a pink flower in her hair. Eddie didn't say much. He was so nervous that his tongue was glued to his teeth. But they danced to the music of a big band, and he bought her a lemon soda and a bag of candy. She had to go home before her parents got angry, but as she walked away, she turned and waved.

That was Eddie's true-love moment. For the rest of his life, whenever he thought of Marguerite, he pictured that scene. He saw her as she turned and waved, her dark hair falling over one eye, and each time he felt his heart bursting with love again.

On the night he met Marguerite, he came home and woke his older brother. He told him he'd met the girl he was going to marry.

"Shut up and go to sleep, Eddie," his brother complained.

Sixteen minutes to live. Eddie watched a wave break on the beach. He used to think a lot about Marguerite, but not so much now. She was hidden somewhere, like an old wound under a bandage, and he had grown more used to the bandage.

♦

No story exists by itself. Sometimes stories meet at corners or cover each other completely, like stones beneath a river.

The end of Eddie's story was touched by another seemingly unrelated story that happened months earlier on a cloudy night when a young man arrived at Ruby Park with three of his friends. Nicky, the young man, had just passed his driving test and had his dad's car for the evening. He put the car key in his jacket pocket, and then he tied the jacket around his waist.

For the next few hours, Nicky and his friends rode all the fastest rides, shouting and throwing their hands in the air. Later they returned to the car lot, exhausted and laughing, drinking cans of beer which they'd hidden in brown paper bags. Nicky reached into his jacket pocket. He cursed.

The key was gone.

♦

Fourteen minutes until his death. Because of his bad leg, Eddie hadn't walked easily since the war, but back at the Stardust Room with Marguerite he had still moved smoothly and skilfully. He squeezed his eyes shut to bring those memories closer. He could almost hear the band playing his favorite song: "You made me love you …"

Twelve minutes to live.

"Excuse me."

A little girl, maybe eight years old, stood in front of him, blocking his sunlight. He recognized the girl, with her blond curls and a T-shirt with Donald Duck on the front. Amy, he thought her name was. Amy or Annie. She'd been there a lot this summer, although Eddie never saw a parent with her.

"Excuse me," she said again. "Eddie Maintenance?"

"Just Eddie, please."

"Eddie, can you make me …"

"Tell me, kid. I don't have all day."

"Can you make me an animal? Please? *Can you?*"

Eddie reached into his pocket and brought out a balloon that he carried for this purpose. He began to blow up the balloon and asked, "Where are your parents?"

"My mom's on one of the rides with her boyfriend."

Eddie understood. With a few neat twists he turned the balloon into a rabbit with a head, ears, body, and tail.

"Oh, thank you!"

As the girl ran off, Eddie closed his eyes and tried to get the old song back into his head.

♦

How do people choose their final words? Do they realize how important those words may be? Is everyone wise at the end?

By his eighty-third birthday, Eddie had lost nearly everyone he cared about. He believed that when your time came, it came. You might say something smart on your way out, but you might say something stupid.

Eddie's final words would be, "Get back!"

♦

Here are the sounds of Eddie's last minutes on Earth. Waves crashing on the beach. The heavy beat of rock music. The sound of a small airplane engine. And this:

"OH, MY GOD! LOOK!"

Eddie recognized the sound of an emergency.

"LOOK! LOOK!"

A fat woman holding a shopping bag was pointing and screaming. A small crowd gathered around her, their eyes to the skies.

Eddie saw the problem immediately. At the top of Freddy's Free Fall, the new "tower drop" attraction, one of the cars had come out of line and was now leaning dangerously, ready to throw the four passengers into the air. The two men and two women, held only by the safety bar, were desperately trying to find something to hold onto.

"OH, MY GOD!" the fat woman screamed. "THOSE PEOPLE! THEY'RE GOING TO FALL! THEY'RE GOING TO BE KILLED!"

People ran up from the beach, pointing at the sky. "Look!

One of the rides has gone crazy!" Eddie rushed to the safety fence at the base of the ride as fast as he could.

Freddy's Free Fall was supposed to drop two cars in a stomach-turning dive, and then be stopped at the last second by a powerful burst of air. How did one car come loose like that? It was hanging just a few feet below the upper platform, at the beginning of the drop.

Eddie reached the gate and had to catch his breath. Dominguez came running and nearly banged into him.

Eddie caught his arm and said, "Listen! Who's up there?"

"Willie."

"OK. I think he hit the emergency stop button. That's why the car is hanging. Get the ladder and tell Willie to unhook the safety bar so those people can get out. OK? He'll have to do it from the back of the car, so you need to hold him while he leans out there, OK? Then, the two of you get those people out. One holds the other! Understood? ... *Understood!?* Then send that car down so we can see what happened!"

Eddie watched nervously as Dominguez hurried up the ladder. Although his park had been free of any serious accidents, Eddie knew the horror stories of his business. Once, in Brighton, a screw came unfastened on a Ferris wheel and two people fell to their death. Another time, in Wonderland Park, a man tried to walk across the roller coaster line; he fell through and got stuck from his chest down. He saw the cars racing toward him and ... well, that was the worst.

There were people all around Eddie now, watching in horror as Willie and Dominguez worked. Eddie was thinking about the mechanical parts of Freddy's Free Fall. He was trying to imagine how the machine could go wrong.

"Wait ..." Eddie said to himself. "Cable ..." he whispered.

Above him, Willie lifted the safety bar and the riders were quickly pulled to the platform. The crowd cheered, but Eddie's mind was somewhere else. "The cable is coming apart ..." he thought, and he was right. For the last few months, the cable that lifted Car Number 2 had been rubbing against a locked pulley, which little by little ate into the cable's steel wires. It was impossible to see the problem unless you managed to get inside the machine.

But why had the pulley become locked? Its movement had been blocked by a small object that had fallen into the machinery.

A car key.

"Don't release the car!" Eddie screamed. He waved his arms to get Dominguez's attention. "HEY! IT'S THE CABLE! DON'T RELEASE THE CAR! THE CABLE WILL BREAK!"

But Dominguez and Willie could only hear the wild cheers from the crowd as they unloaded the passengers onto the platform. Eddie looked up and saw Willie put his finger on the green button to release the car.

"NO, NO, NO, DON'T!"

Then Eddie turned to the crowd. "GET BACK!"

Something in Eddie's voice alarmed the people; they stopped cheering and began to run. An opening cleared around the bottom of Freddy's Free Fall.

And Eddie saw the last face of his life.

The little girl—Amy? Annie?—had fallen over the ride's metal base. Her nose was running and tears filled her eyes. She was still holding her balloon rabbit.

"Ma ... Mom ... Mom," she cried.

Eddie looked from the girl up to the ride. Did he have time? The cars were dropping, and for Eddie everything became very clear. He pushed forward on his bad leg and ignored the terrible pain that almost knocked him down. He took a big step. Then another. He looked up and saw the cable break. Car Number 2 was falling with nothing to stop it.

In those final seconds, Eddie seemed to hear the whole world:

9

screams, waves, music, the wind, and a low ugly sound that he realized was his own voice bursting through his chest. The little girl raised her arms. Eddie dived toward her, landing on the metal platform, which split open his shirt and then his skin just below the pocket that read EDDIE and MAINTENANCE. He felt two hands in his own—two small hands.

A sudden crash.

A blinding flash of light.

And then, nothing.

Chapter 2
The First Person Eddie Meets in Heaven

Eddie didn't notice much in his final moment on Earth. He didn't notice the crowd of people or even the car from Freddy's Free Fall as it crashed down on top of him. In his last few seconds all he saw was the little girl lying on the metal base of the ride where she had fallen. He reached out for her—then nothing. And nothing happened afterward. It wasn't like a scene from a TV movie. Eddie didn't float above the park and watch what was going on. He didn't suddenly come alive again. No, Eddie, it appeared, was really and truly dead.

"Where …? Where am I?" Eddie asked himself.

Then he *was* floating—through different bright colors. Very calmly, Eddie began to question what had happened. The car was falling and the little girl was crying. What was her name? Amy? Annie? He remembered feeling two small hands in his.

"Did I save her?" he wondered. He was desperate to know.

Eddie floated through more colors and suddenly he thought: "Nothing hurts!"

All of his aches and pains had disappeared. And this included his mental sufferings; Eddie no longer felt any sadness or worry or regret. He dropped from the sky into an enormous pool of water, and still he was not anxious or afraid. He went underwater and everything was completely silent.

He kept asking himself, "Where's my worry? Where's my pain?"

♦

Today is Eddie's Birthday

It is the 1920s. In a crowded hospital in one of the poorest sections of the city, Eddie's father is in the waiting room, with a group of expectant fathers. They are all smoking cigarettes and walking in circles around the room, waiting for news of their wives and babies.

A nurse comes in and finds Eddie's father. "Congratulations," she says. "You have a healthy baby boy."

The nurse leads the new father down the hall to the babies' room. She goes from one tiny bed to the next. Finally, she stops and picks up one of the babies. She holds him up for his father to see.

The father takes a deep breath and smiles.

His.

♦

Eddie became conscious again in an enormous teacup. It was part of an old Ruby Park ride that he had known as a child. Eddie reached out to find his cane, which he always needed to help him out of bed in the morning. He couldn't see the cane, but when he tried to pull himself up, he realized that he didn't need it. Neither his back nor his leg hurt. He jumped out of the teacup ride like a small child. He had three quick thoughts:

First, he felt wonderful.

Second, he was alone.

Third, he was still at Ruby Park.

But this wasn't the Ruby Park where he had died. This

11

was the amusement park of his childhood, with big tents, lots of grass, salt-water swimming pools, and a clear view of the ocean. The rides were old-fashioned, but they all looked new and freshly painted in bright red and white. Beyond the park he could see the crowded streets of his old neighborhood, alive with kids playing games in the street.

Eddie tried to shout but he couldn't make a sound. This was strange, but it was even stranger that his body felt so extraordinary. He walked, then he jumped. No pain. On the outside, he still looked like an eighty-three-year-old man in a brown maintenance uniform. But his body felt young and strong—and he could do anything! He touched his toes, he did a little dance, and then he ran!

Running! Eddie hadn't really and truly run in more than sixty years. Now he was running as fast as he had run as a young boy. He sped past the old rides, past the French carousel with its beautiful wooden horses and glass mirrors, and along the boardwalk. After every few steps, he held out his arms and jumped, like he was trying to fly. It was a strange sight to see an old man moving so fast and so smoothly. But the running boy is inside every man, however old he gets.

And then Eddie stopped running. He heard a voice. Someone was speaking very loudly into a microphone.

"What do you think, ladies and gentlemen? Have you ever seen such a terrible sight?" shouted a man on a stage.

Eddie looked up at the sign above the man. It read:
The World's Oddest Citizens!
Ruby Park's Freak Show!

Eddie remembered the Freak Show, but he knew it had been shut down at least fifty years ago, at about the time when television had become popular and viewers could see strange things from around the world. Eddie had met some of the Park's Odd Citizens when he was a child and his father was

12

the maintenance man. A woman with a beard, a man who swallowed swords, a rubber man, a fat woman. Eddie had felt sorry for these people. They had to sit on a stage for hours every day while people stared at them. And all the time, the master of ceremonies talked about how odd they were.

"Come and see the freaks! But are they really human? Come inside and take a close look, then judge for yourself."

Eddie walked through the entrance into the dark hall. He could still hear the man with the microphone: "This tragic man has had to live a lifetime as a freak ... Come in and see his terrible condition for yourself."

The curtain opened and the man outside stopped shouting. In the silence, Eddie could see that there was only one person on the stage, sitting in a chair, staring out at his audience. He was a middle-aged man with short hair, narrow shoulders, and a sad face. Eddie would not have remembered this "Odd Citizen," except for one important feature.

The man's skin was blue.

"Hello, Edward," the man said. "I've been waiting for you."

♦

"Don't be afraid ..." the Blue Man said calmly and quietly, rising slowly from his chair.

Eddie could only stare. He remembered the Blue Man from when he was a child, but he hadn't really known him. Why was he seeing him now? He was like a face that might appear in a dream and the next morning you say, "You'll never guess who I dreamed about last night."

"Your body feels like a child's, right?" the Blue Man asked.

Eddie tried to speak but no sound came out.

"You were a child when you knew me, so you start here with the same feelings and memories that you had then."

"Start *what*?" Eddie thought to himself.

13

The Blue Man lifted his chin. His skin was an unnatural shade of blue, like an old blueberry that was beginning to turn gray. He walked outside and Eddie followed. They stood looking at an empty boardwalk and an empty beach. Eddie wondered if the whole planet was empty.

"Tell me something, Edward," the Blue Man said. He pointed to a wooden roller coaster in the distance. Its name, The Whipper, was painted on the sign at the entrance to the ride. "Is The Whipper still 'the fastest ride on Earth'?"

Eddie shook his head no. These days you could only see one of those in a museum. It would look very old-fashioned and unbelievably slow next to modern roller coasters.

"Of course not," the Blue Man said. "But things don't change here. And I'm afraid we don't sit up here looking through the clouds, watching what's going on down there."

"Up here?" Eddie thought.

The Blue Man smiled, appearing to have heard a question. He touched Eddie's shoulder and Eddie sensed a feeling of warmth unlike anything he had ever felt before. Suddenly, he thought of more questions.

"How did I die?" he thought to himself.

"An accident," the Blue Man said.

"How long have I been dead?"

"A minute. An hour. A thousand years."

"Where am I?"

The Blue Man pointed at everything around them, and Ruby Park came back to life. The Ferris Wheel began to spin, the bumper cars crashed into each other, the roller coaster sped down its steep path, and the horses on the beautiful French carousel went up and down to the cheerful amusement park music. People were laughing and talking, the ocean was in front of them, and the sky was the color of lemons.

"We're in heaven," the Blue Man said.

"No, no!" Eddie thought. "This isn't heaven. It can't be!"

"Why can't this be heaven?" the Blue Man asked. "Is it because it's the place where you grew up?"

Eddie tried to say, "Yes!"

"Well," the Blue Man began, "heaven can be found in very unlikely corners. And heaven has many steps. This, for me, is the second—and for you it's the first."

"Heaven?" Eddie thought. "Impossible." For Eddie, this was an old amusement park, that was all. It was a place to scream and get wet and waste your money on rides and games. The idea that this was heaven was beyond his imagination. He wanted to say this to the Blue Man, but he still couldn't speak.

"Your voice will come. You can't talk when you first arrive." The Blue Man smiled. "It helps you listen."

♦

"There are five people you meet in heaven," the Blue Man explained. "Each of us was in your life for a reason. Maybe you didn't know the reason at the time, and that is what heaven is for. For understanding your life on Earth." Eddie looked confused. "People have an idea about heaven. They think it's something like a big garden, a place where you can float on clouds, swim in beautiful lakes, sit on top of perfect mountains. But life after death is not peaceful and happy without meaning and understanding. God's greatest gift to you is the understanding of what happened in your life on Earth. Then you will find the peace you have been searching for."

Again, Eddie tried to speak. He was tired of being silent.

"Edward, I am your first person. When I died, I met five people who explained my life to me, and then I came here to wait for you, to stand in your line, to tell you my story, which becomes part of yours. There will be four people after me. Some you knew, maybe some you didn't. But they all crossed

15

your path before you died. And they affected your life forever."

Eddie tried his hardest to speak. "What ...?" he finally managed to say. "What ... killed ...?" The Blue Man waited patiently. "What ... killed ... you?"

The Blue Man looked a bit surprised. He smiled at Eddie.

"You did," he said.

♦

Today is Eddie's Birthday

Eddie is squeezing his new baseball, his gift for his seventh birthday. He imagines he is one of his heroes, maybe Walter Johnson, one of the greatest baseball players of all time.

"Hey, Eddie, throw it to me," his brother, Joe, shouts. "Come on, Eddie. Share."

They are running along the boardwalk, heading toward the street to play baseball with their friends. Eddie stops and imagines he is a professional baseball player. He throws the ball hard and straight.

"Too hard!" Joe shouts, as he jumps away from the ball. The boys watch it go toward the tents at the back of Ruby Park.

"Come on, Joe. Help me find my ball," Eddie calls.

The two boys are on their hands and knees, searching for the ball, when an enormous woman and a very hairy man with a beard that reaches his belt come out of one of the tents. Freaks from the freak show.

The children freeze.

"What do you think you're doing here?" the hairy man says, smiling, but with an evil look in his eyes. "Are you looking for trouble?"

Joe starts to cry. He jumps up and runs away as fast as he can.

Eddie gets up but moves slowly toward the freaks. His ball is near the man's feet.

"This is mine," he whispers. He seizes the ball and runs after his brother.

16

♦

"Listen, mister," Eddie said very slowly. "I never killed you, OK? I don't even *know* you."

"Well, let me tell you my story. My name is Joseph Corvelzchik. When I was a small boy, my family and I came to this country from a small village in Poland. It was 1894 and we were poor immigrants. We slept on the floor in my uncle's kitchen, and my father got a job in a factory, sewing buttons on coats. When I was ten years old, he took me out of school to work in the factory with him."

Eddie was listening, but he wondered why the Blue Man was telling him this.

"I was a nervous child, and the noise on the factory floor made things worse. I was too young to be there with all of the men swearing and complaining and making jokes I didn't understand. Whenever the boss came near, my father told me to look down: 'Don't make him notice you.' But once I dropped a sack of buttons when the boss was near me. He screamed at me, and said I was a worthless child. He said I had to get out of his factory. I can still see the moment when my father begged him not to fire me, and the boss just laughed in his face. I was afraid for my father and for my whole family. My stomach was twisting and turning in pain. Then I felt something wet on my leg. I looked down. The boss pointed at my wet pants and laughed even louder.

"After that, my father refused to speak to me. He was ashamed of me, of what I had done in front of his boss and the men in the factory. My father's attitude toward me ruined my life. I wet the bed at night because I was so nervous, and when my father found out, I saw disappointment in his eyes.

"You see, Edward, I was not always a freak—just a nervous kid with a father who was always worried about money, and

17

that made him cruel. I eventually went to a drugstore and asked for something to calm my nerves. Medicine wasn't very modern back then, and I was given silver nitrate. Silver nitrate. Do you know that scientists later discovered that it was poison? But back then I took it every night, waiting for it to work. But it didn't, so I took more of it, more often.

"Soon people were staring at me. My skin was turning gray. This made me more nervous, so I took more silver nitrate, until my skin went from gray to blue. I was working in a different factory, but the boss fired me. He said I was scaring the other workers with my blue skin. Without work, how would I eat? Where would I live?

"Then, one night, I was in a dark bar down by the boardwalk. I didn't think anyone would notice me there, but a man with a wooden leg saw me and came for a chat. He was with a group of freaks from Ruby Park, and he thought there might be a job for me as one of the Odd Citizens.

"Next day, I had a new job at Ruby Park. I didn't have to do much, just sit on the stage, half undressed, as people walked past and the man with the microphone told them how unusual, how heart-breaking my life was. But I had a life. I lived above an Italian café. I played cards at night with the other freaks and Ruby Park employees, sometimes even with your father. In the early mornings, if I wore a long shirt and a big hat, I could walk along this beach without scaring people. It may not sound like much, but for me it was the first real freedom I had ever known." He stopped and looked at Eddie. "Do you understand why you've met me *here*? This is not *your* heaven. It's mine."

♦

Take one story, viewed through two different pairs of eyes.

It's a rainy Sunday morning in July, in the late 1920s. Eddie and his friends are playing baseball with the ball that Eddie got for his birthday almost a year ago. One of the boys hits the ball over Eddie's head and it flies into the street. Eddie runs after the ball and into the path of a car. The car comes to a sudden stop and misses the boy by a few inches. Eddie lets out a deep breath, picks up the ball, and races back to his friends. The game soon ends and the children run to the arcade.

But someone else would see this story very differently. A man is behind the wheel of a car. He's just learning to drive and has borrowed a friend's car to practice. The road is wet from the morning rain. Suddenly, a baseball flies into the street and a boy races after it. The driver steps on the brakes and turns the wheel sharply. The car slides to a stop and the boy escapes unharmed.

The man somehow calms down enough to drive away, but he is very upset, thinking of how close he came to tragedy. His heart, which isn't strong, is beating wildly, and he feels exhausted by the experience. He can't see properly and his head drops for a moment. His car almost runs into another car, so our man turns his wheel sharply again and lets his vehicle roll until it runs into the back of a parked truck. There is a small crashing noise. The man's head falls forward and hits the wheel with enough force to make his forehead bleed. He steps out of the car and looks at the damage, but he doesn't have the strength to stay standing up. His chest hurts and he has a terrible pain in his left arm. It's Sunday morning and the street is empty and quiet. He sinks to the sidewalk beside the car and leans against it. An hour passes. A policeman finds him and he is taken to a hospital. A doctor writes the report: *died from a heart attack*. No relatives can be found.

Take one story and look at it through two different pairs of eyes. It is the same day, the same moment, but one person thinks the story ends happily, at an arcade, putting pennies into a machine. The other person finishes his day in a hospital, with

19

a conversation between two young doctors.

"Did you see the dead body they just brought in?" one says.

"No. Anything interesting?"

"His skin was blue. Really bright blue! I've never seen anything like it."

"Do you understand?" the Blue Man said, after telling his story. "Little boy?"

Eddie suddenly realized.

"Oh no," he whispered.

♦

Today is Eddie's Birthday

He is eight years old. He's sitting on the couch with his arms crossed in anger. His mother is tying his shoes. His father is looking in the mirror, fixing his tie.

"I don't WANT to go," Eddie says.

"I know," his mother says, not looking up, "but we have to. Everyone from Ruby Park is going. Sometimes you have to do things when sad things happen."

"But it's my BIRTHDAY." Eddie stares at the box with his new model airplane. He wants to stay at home and put it together. He is good at building things, and wants to show it to his friends at a birthday party. Instead, they have to get dressed up and go someplace. It isn't fair, he thinks.

"Enough complaining!" his father shouts. He gives Eddie an angry look. Eddie goes silent.

At the cemetery Eddie recognizes some of the workers from Ruby Park. He watches a man shovel dirt into a hole. The man says something about dust to dust. Eddie holds his mother's hand and secretly begins to count. He's supposed to be sad, but he hopes that by the time he reaches a thousand, he will have his birthday back.

♦

THE FIRST LESSON

"Please, mister ..." Eddie begged. "I didn't know. Believe me ... God help me, I didn't know."

"I understand," the Blue Man said. "You couldn't know. You were too young."

"But now I have to pay—is that right? Now you're going to punish me for causing your death?"

"No, Edward. That's not why we're having this meeting. You're here so I can teach you something. All the people you meet here have one thing to teach you."

Eddie wasn't sure he understood. He was still waiting for his punishment. "What are you going to teach me?" he asked.

"I want you to understand that there are no random acts. We are all connected. You cannot separate one life from another. That would be like separating a breath of air from the wind."

Eddie tried to understand. "We were throwing a *ball*. Because I was stupid and ran into the street after my ball, you died. Why should *you* have to die because of *me*? It isn't *fair*."

"But, Eddie, fairness doesn't govern life and death. If it did, no good person would ever die young.

"Let's go back to the cemetery and look at the people at my funeral. I didn't know many of them very well, but they came. Why do you think they did? It is because the human spirit knows, deep down, that all lives are connected. Death doesn't just take someone, it also misses someone else, and in that small distance between being taken and being missed, lives are changed.

"Are you wondering why you didn't die instead of me? But during my time on Earth, other people died instead of me, too. It happens every day. Maybe lightning strikes a minute after you are gone, or an airplane crashes after you decided not to take that flight. A friend gets sick and you don't. These things are not random. There is a balance to everything. One dies, another grows. Birth and death are part of a whole."

Eddie looked at the Blue Man's funeral. He wondered about his own funeral. Had there been one? Had anyone come?

"I still don't understand," Eddie whispered. "What good came from your death?"

"You lived," the Blue Man answered.

"But we hardly knew each other. What if I had been a stranger?"

"Strangers," the Blue Man said, "are just family you haven't gotten to know yet."

With those words, the Blue Man pulled Eddie close. Immediately, Eddie felt everything the Blue Man had felt in his life—his loneliness, his shame, his nervousness, his failures, even his heart attack—swim into his body. Then it felt like a drawer being closed.

"I am leaving," the Blue Man whispered. "This step of heaven has finished for me. But there are others for you to meet."

"Wait," Eddie said. "Please tell me. Did I save the little girl? At the park. Did I save her?" He was disappointed when the Blue Man didn't answer. "Then my death was a waste, just like my life."

"No life is a waste," the Blue Man said. "The only time we waste is the time that we spend thinking we are alone."

He walked back toward the cemetery and smiled. As he did, his skin turned from blue to a beautiful shade of light brown— it was the most perfect skin Eddie had ever seen.

"Wait!" Eddie shouted, but he was suddenly lifted into the air, away from the cemetery and out over the ocean. He looked down at Ruby Park.

Then it was gone.

♦

Back at Ruby Park, the crowd stood silently around what remained of Freddy's Free Fall. Old women felt afraid. Mothers pulled their children away from the wreck. Men with strong arms pushed through the crowd to see if there was something they could do, but they saw that it was useless. Everyone watched, helpless in the hot sun.

"How bad is it?" people whispered. From the back of the crowd, Dominguez burst through, his face red, his maintenance shirt dirty with oil. He saw the wreck.

"No, no, Eddie," he cried, holding his head. Other park workers arrived. They pushed people back. But then, they, too, didn't know what to do. They stood with their hands in their pockets, waiting for the ambulances. The mothers, the fathers, the kids with their extra-large soda cups—everyone was too shocked to look and too shocked to leave. Death was at their feet, as cheerful music from the arcades and from the park rides filled the air.

Ambulances and police cars arrived. Men in uniforms stretched yellow tape around the area. Everything in the park closed. Word spread across the beach of the tragic thing that had happened, and by sunset Ruby Park was empty.

♦

Today is Eddie's Birthday

From his bedroom, even with the door closed, Eddie can smell the steak his mother is grilling with green peppers and sweet red onions. It's his favorite meal, a special supper for his seventeenth birthday.

"Eddie!" his mother shouts from the kitchen. "Where are you? Everyone's here!"

He rolls off the bed and joins his mother, father, and brother Joe in the living room.

"There's the birthday boy," his mother cries happily as Eddie walks

23

shyly into the room. He wears a white shirt and blue tie, which feels tight on his strong neck. Several friends from Ruby Park and some cousins from Romania raise their glasses and shout, "Happy Birthday, Eddie!" His father is playing cards in the corner, in a small cloud of cigarette smoke.

"Hey, Mom, guess what?" Joe shouts. "Eddie met a girl last night at the Stardust Room. Said he's going to marry her."

"Shut up," Eddie says to Joe.

Joe ignores him. "He came into the bedroom all dreamy and he said, 'Joe, I met the girl I'm going to marry!'"

Eddie turns red. "I said shut your mouth!"

Now the questions start from the other people in the room. "What's her name, Eddie?" "Does she go to church?" "Is she pretty?"

"He's in love," Joe shouts.

"SHUT UP!" Eddie shouts back and then hits his brother on the chin.

The two brothers struggle with each other until their father puts his cards down and shouts, "Stop it, you two, before I whip both of you."

The brothers separate, breathing hard and staring at each other. One of their aunts whispers, "I think Eddie really likes this girl."

Later, after the steak has been eaten, the birthday cake has been cut, and the guests have gone home, Eddie's mother turns on the radio. There is news about the war in Europe, and Eddie's father says something about a bad time for amusement parks.

"Such awful news," Eddie's mother says. "Not at a birthday party." She changes the radio station and finds a music program. A band is playing dance music, and she smiles and sings to it. Then she takes Eddie by the hand and pulls him out of his chair.

"Show me how you danced with your new friend," she says.

"Mom, no."

"Come on."

Unwillingly, Eddie stands and begins dancing with his mother. His brother laughs.

24

But soon Eddie and his mother are moving smoothly around the living room. Eddie is already about six inches taller than his mother, but she leads him effortlessly.

"So," she whispers, "you like this girl."

Eddie finds it hard to speak.

"It's all right," she says. "I'm happy for you."

They spin to the table and Eddie's mother pulls Joe up.

"Now you two dance," she says.

"With him? Mom!"

But she orders them to dance, and soon Joe and Eddie are laughing and joking around. They join hands and move in exaggerated circles. Around and around they go with their delighted mother watching them.

Chapter 3
The Second Person Eddie Meets in Heaven

Eddie felt his feet touch the ground. The color of the sky was changing from bright blue to dark gray. He was in a forest that had been destroyed by fire. He touched his arms, shoulders, and legs. He felt stronger than before, but when he tried to touch his toes, he couldn't do it. He wasn't a child any longer, but he was strong and felt powerful.

He looked at the lifeless earth around him. He could see a wrecked wagon and the dried bones of a dead animal on a hill close to him. A hot wind hit him in the face. The sky exploded into a bright, blinding yellow.

And, again, Eddie ran.

He ran differently now, with the controlled steps of a soldier. He heard something like thunder—explosions, or bombs bursting—and he fell to the ground without thinking, landed on his stomach, and pulled himself along on his elbows. Suddenly, it began to rain, a thick, brownish flood from the sky. Eddie put his head down and dragged himself along in the mud, trying to keep the dirty water out of his mouth.

Finally, his head hit something solid. He looked up and saw a rifle stuck in the ground with a helmet sitting on top of it and a soldier's set of dog tags hanging from the helmet. He reached up and wrapped his wet fingers around the dog tags before taking shelter from the rain under a few leaves that were left on the nearest tree. He sat in the darkness and tried to catch his breath. Fear had found him, even in heaven.

The name on the dog tags was his.

◆

Young men go to war—sometimes because they have to, sometimes because they want to. Always, they feel they are supposed to. How do we explain war? Are soldiers courageous because they pick up guns? Are they cowards because they lay them down?

When his country entered the war, Eddie woke up early one rainy morning, shaved, combed his hair, left the house, and signed up for the army. Others were fighting. He would, too.

Since he had never fired an actual rifle, Eddie began to practice at the shooting arcade at Ruby Park after work. He put nickel after nickel into the shooting games, aiming at the metal lions and tigers. He had taken the job at Ruby Park to save money to study engineering. That was his goal—he wanted to build things, even if his brother Joe was always saying, "Eddie, you aren't smart enough for that."

On one of his final nights at home, Eddie was at the shooting arcade. *Bang!* He tried to imagine that he was shooting at the enemy. *Bang!*

"Practicing to kill, are you, son?"

Mickey Shea, one of his dad's card-playing friends from Ruby Park, was standing behind him. Eddie could smell that the older man had been drinking. He didn't answer and returned to his shooting. *Bang!* Another hit. *Bang!* Another.

Mickey's hand came down heavily onto Eddie's shoulder. "Listen to me, boy. War isn't a game. If you see the enemy, you fire and you don't think about who you're shooting or killing or why, do you hear me? No hesitation. No guilt. You want to come home again, so you just fire, you don't think."

He squeezed Eddie's shoulder even harder. "Remember: Don't think. That's what gets you killed."

Mickey gave the teenager's arm a final squeeze before walking away with tears in his eyes. Eddie watched him go and thought about what he had said.

Young men go to war—sometimes because they have to, sometimes because they want to. A few days later, Eddie packed his bag and left Ruby Park behind.

♦

The rain stopped. Eddie looked out from under the tree and saw the rifle and helmet still stuck in the ground. He remembered why soldiers did this: it marked the graves of their dead. He came out on his knees. Away in the distance, he could see what remained of a village that had been bombed and burned. For a moment, Eddie stared. Then his chest felt tight, like a man who had just heard some bad news. This place. He knew it. He had seen it for years in his worst dreams.

"Not a healthy place," a voice suddenly said from somewhere above Eddie. "Lots of diseases around here, but I died here as healthy as a horse."

Eddie looked around him. "Come out," he said.

"Come up," the voice said.

And in a flash, Eddie was in the tree, near the top, and the tree was as tall as an office building. He was sitting on a big branch with the Earth far below him. Through the smaller branches and leaves, he could see the shadowy figure of a man in an army uniform. The man's face was covered with a dark oil. His eyes shone like tiny red light bulbs.

Eddie swallowed hard. "Captain?" he whispered.

Eddie had served under the Captain in the army. They fought together in the Philippines, and Eddie had heard that his commanding officer had died in battle.

"Have they explained the rules to you, soldier?"

"I'm dead," he said.

"You're right about that."

"And *you're* dead. And you're … my second person."

"Right again. I bet you didn't expect me, did you?"

◆

Eddie learned many things during the war. He learned how to fire a real rifle. He learned to shave with cold water in his helmet. He learned to smoke. He learned to march. He learned to cross a river on a rope bridge while carrying a heavy coat, a radio, a rifle, a backpack, food, and water. He learned how to drink the worst coffee he had ever tasted. He learned a few words in a few foreign languages. He learned how depressing it was to realize that the fighting does not stop after one victory, but that there is another battle and then another.

He learned to whistle through his teeth. He learned to sleep on rocky earth. He learned to live with insects in his dirty clothes. He learned that a man's bones really do look white when they burst through the skin.

He learned to pray quickly. He learned to keep a photograph of Marguerite and his letters to her and to his family inside his helmet, where they could be found by the other soldiers if he was killed. He learned that you could be talking to your friend one minute, whispering about how hungry you are, and in the next minute see him fall forward, hit by an enemy bullet.

He learned that even officers talk in their sleep the night before a battle. He learned how to take a prisoner, although he never learned how to become one. Then one night, on a Philippine island, he heard one of his friends crying beside him as they hid from the enemy. "Shut up, will you?" Eddie shouted. Then he saw that there was an enemy soldier standing beside his friend with a rifle pointed at his friend's head. Eddie suddenly felt something cold at his neck, and knew that there was an enemy soldier behind him, too.

♦

The Captain was older than the men under him. He was a career man in the army. Most of his men liked him well enough, although he had a short temper. But the Captain always promised he would "leave no one behind," no matter what happened, and his men trusted him because of that.

"Captain …" Eddie began. "You look …"

"Like the last time you saw me?" He smiled at the confused look on Eddie's face.

"I still don't know why I'm here. I had a nothing life. I lived in the same apartment for years. I took care of amusement park rides, from roller coasters to stupid little space ships. I just floated through life. Do you know what I'm talking about, Captain?" Eddie swallowed. "What am I doing here?"

The Captain looked at him with his shining red eyes, and Eddie stopped himself from asking the question that he wondered about after his experience with the Blue Man: Did he kill the Captain, too?

"I've been wondering," the Captain said, rubbing his chin. "How about the guys from our company: Willingham? Morton? Smitty? Did you ever see any of them after the war?"

Eddie remembered the names. The truth was, they had not had any contact. War had pulled them together, but it had also

29

pushed them apart. The things they saw, the things they did—
sometimes soldiers just wanted to forget.

"To be honest, sir, I didn't. Sorry."

The Captain had expected that. "And you? Did you go back
to the amusement park, where we all promised to go if we got
out alive? Free rides for soldiers? Isn't that what you said?"

Eddie nearly smiled. That was what he said. What they all
said. But when the war ended, nobody came.

"Yeah, I went back," Eddie said. "And ... I never left. I
made plans ... but my leg held me back. I don't know. Nothing
happened the way I wanted."

The Captain studied Eddie's face. Then in a serious voice,
he asked, "Do you still juggle?"

♦

"GO! ... YOU GO! ... YOU GO!"

The enemy soldiers screamed at them, pushing them along
with their rifles. Eddie, Smitty, Morton, Rabozzo, and the
Captain were forced down a steep hill, hands on their heads.
Gunfire exploded around them. Eddie saw a soldier run
through the trees, then fall in a shower of bullets.

As they marched in the darkness, Eddie tried to take a mental
photograph of everything he could see—huts, roads, trees—
knowing that this kind of information would be valuable in
an escape. At the same time, he felt desperate as he began to
understand the short distance between freedom and prison. As
a plane flew past in the distance, he imagined jumping up and
catching the wing, flying away from this mistake.

But there was no escape. Instead, he and the others were
tied at the wrists and ankles. They were thrown into a hut
in the middle of the Philippine forest. This rough jail sat on
top of shaky poles, keeping the prisoners above the muddy
ground, and they remained there for days, weeks, months,

forced to sleep on the floor with only a few old grain sacks to cover them. A big jar in one corner was their toilet. At night, the enemy guards sat under the hut, listening to their conversations. As time passed, the prisoners said less and less. They grew thin and weak on brown soup with grass and an occasional insect floating in it and rice balls filled with salt.

The enemy soldiers seemed unsure of what to do with them. Sometimes they entered the hut and waved their knives around, shouting in a foreign language, waiting for answers. There were only four of them, and the Captain guessed that they had gotten separated from a larger company, as often happens in war. They were thin and young; one looked too young to be a soldier. The Captain called them Crazy One, Crazy Two, Crazy Three, and Crazy Four.

"We don't want to know their names," he said. "And we don't want them to know ours."

Eddie got angrier and angrier. He was patient, after years at Ruby Park, waiting for rides to finish, but he also wanted revenge, and he wanted to escape. His body felt tight, ready for a fight, and he thought about some of the fights he'd been in back in his old neighborhood. One time, he sent two kids to the hospital after he attacked them with a garbage can lid. What would he do if the guards didn't have guns and knives?

Then, one morning, the prisoners were awakened by the four Crazies and led to a coal mine, where they were forced to work to help the enemy's war effort. There were other prisoners there, too, but each day the number was reduced. The men were given a cup of water every few hours and very little food. By the end of the day, the prisoners' faces were black and their necks and shoulders ached from the back-breaking work.

Then, during the fourth month, Rabozzo developed sores

on his skin and had terrible stomach pains. He could hardly stand up in the mine. The four Crazies showed no pity. They shouted at him and hit him with sticks to keep him working.

"Stop it," Eddie said in a low voice.

Crazy Two, the cruelest of the guards, hit Eddie with the end of his rifle. Eddie fell and a pain spread from shoulder to shoulder. Rabozzo tried to pick up his shovel, but he fell to the floor. Crazy Two screamed at him.

"He's sick!" Eddie shouted, struggling to his feet.

Crazy Two hit Eddie again.

"Shut up, Eddie," Morton whispered. "For your own good."

Crazy Two leaned over Rabozzo. He smiled at the sick man and talked to him softly, like a mother talking to her baby. He smiled when he looked up and saw everyone watching him. Then he pulled a gun out of his belt, pushed it into Rabozzo's ear, and shot him in the head.

Nobody moved. Crazy Two shouted something into Eddie's face and waved his gun at him. Crazy Three and Four pulled Rabozzo's body along the mine floor, leaving a stream of blood behind.

After that, Eddie stopped praying. Instead of dreaming of home, he and the Captain started talking about how to escape before they were shot like Rabozzo. They noticed that each day there were fewer prisoners working in the mine. Each night, they could hear bombing; it seemed to be getting closer. The Captain guessed that the Crazies were desperate and would think of leaving soon, too, but before they left, they would destroy everything and kill the few remaining prisoners.

Three weeks later, under a sky with a full moon, Crazy Three was on guard duty. He had two large rocks, almost the size of baseballs, and because he was bored, he was trying to juggle with them. He kept dropping them, picking them up, trying again. Eddie had been asleep, and the annoying noise woke him. But now he looked up and watched Crazy Three. He felt his nerves coming to life. His brain was racing.

"Captain …" he whispered. "You ready to move?"

The Captain raised his head. "What're you thinking?"

"Look at Crazy Three and those rocks. I can juggle."

"What are you talking about?" the Captain asked.

But Eddie was already shouting at the guard. "Hey! You're doing it wrong." He made circles with his hands to show the guard the right way to move the rocks. Eddie held out his hands. "I can juggle. Give me the rocks. I'll show you."

Crazy Three was cautious. Of all the guards, Eddie felt, he had his best chance with this one. Crazy Three occasionally gave the prisoners an extra piece of bread or tried to talk to them in his language. Eddie moved his hands in circles again and smiled. The guard picked up his rifle and then walked over to Eddie with the two rocks.

"Like this," Eddie said, and he began to juggle effortlessly. He had learned from one of the Italian jugglers at Ruby Park—a man who juggled six plates at one time. Eddie had spent hours practicing. Most of the kids around the park were really good at juggling. They did it naturally, without thinking.

Eddie was juggling fast now, making a big impression on Crazy Three. Then he stopped and said, "Get me another one. *Three* rocks, see?" Eddie held up three fingers. "*Three.*"

The Captain, Morton, and Smitty were watching Eddie now.

"Where are you going with this?" Smitty whispered.

"If I can get one more rock …" Eddie whispered back.

Crazy Three opened the door to the hut and did what Eddie had hoped for: He shouted at the other guards. Crazy One came in with another rock and Crazy Two followed him in. With the third rock, Eddie smiled at his audience and signalled for them to sit down. Eddie threw the rocks in a smooth pattern. He sang a song as he juggled. The guards laughed. Eddie laughed. The Captain laughed. Buying time.

"*Get clo-ser*," Eddie sang to the others as the guards began to relax. Eddie threw one rock high into the air, then juggled the lower two, then caught the third, then did it again.

The guards clapped. They were enjoying the show.

Eddie was juggling faster now, throwing the rocks higher and watching the guards' eyes as they followed them into the air. He sang the song, but then added, "*When I count to three ... Captain, the guy on the left ...*"

Crazy Two looked unhappy. Did he suspect something? But Eddie smiled the way the jugglers back at Ruby Park smiled when they were losing their audience. "Watch the rocks! It's the greatest show on Earth," Eddie sang in his happiest, most persuasive voice. Eddie went faster, then counted, "One ... two ..." then threw a rock much higher than before. The Crazies watched it rise.

"Now!" Eddie shouted. In the middle of his juggle, he threw a rock into the face of Crazy Two, breaking his nose. Eddie caught the second rock and hit Crazy One in the chin. Crazy One fell back as the Captain jumped on top of him. Crazy Three froze for a moment and gave Morton and Smitty the chance to get hold of his legs. The door burst open and Crazy Four ran in, and Eddie threw the last rock at him. Crazy Four turned away to avoid the rock, but the Captain was waiting for him with one of the guard's knives. The four guards were killed quickly and violently, using their own weapons.

"For Rabozzo," Smitty whispered.

♦

The prisoners, thin and covered in blood, had expected gunfire from other guards, but the camp was empty.

"Everyone else probably ran off when the bombing started," the Captain whispered. "We're the last group."

They discovered a supply hut and found weapons and flame-throwers. "Let's burn the place down," Morton said.

♦

Today is Eddie's Birthday

Eddie's mother has written "Good luck! Fight Hard!" on the top of the cake, and someone has added the words, "Come home, soon," in blue letters, but the "o-o-n" is squeezed together, so it reads like "son"—"Come home, son."

Eddie's clean clothes and polished shoes are waiting for him in his bedroom, ready for his departure in the morning. The apartment is crowded with family and friends. A three-year-old, one of Eddie's little cousins, points out the kitchen window at the French carousel, which is lit for the evening customers. "Horses!" the child cries. "Pretty horses!"

The front door opens and Eddie hears a voice that makes his heart jump. He wonders if this is a weakness that he shouldn't be taking with him to war.

"Hello, Eddie," Marguerite says as she comes into the room.

She looks wonderful, and Eddie feels that familiar excitement in his chest. She brushes a bit of rainwater from her hair and smiles. She has a small box in her hands.

"I brought you something. For your birthday, and, well … for your leaving, too."

She smiles again. Eddie wants to put his arms around her so badly, he thinks he'll burst. He doesn't care what is in the box. He only wants to remember her holding it out for him. As always, with Marguerite, Eddie mostly wants to freeze time.

"Eddie!" a cousin shouts from the other room. "Come on! Blow out the candles and cut the cake."

Everyone eats and drinks and wishes Eddie good luck, and after the guests have gone home, Eddie walks Marguerite along the boardwalk. They buy sodas and some of their favorite candy. They pick out pieces from the small white bag, playfully fighting each other's fingers. They put their nickels into a few of the arcade games; everyone who works at Ruby Park wishes Eddie good luck. At the end of the evening, they stand on the boardwalk, holding hands and looking out at the ocean. They look like a young couple from a romantic movie.

"You don't have to ask me to wait," Marguerite says.

Eddie swallows. "I don't?"

She shakes her head. Eddie smiles. That question had been worrying him all evening, and now he can pull Marguerite close, making her his. He loves her more in this moment than he thought he could ever love anyone.

A drop of rain hits Eddie's forehead. Then another. He looks up at the clouds. When he looks at Marguerite, there are drops of water on her cheeks. Eddie can't tell if they are raindrops or tears.

"Don't get killed, OK?" she says.

♦

A soldier who has escaped from a prison camp is often full of anger. He thinks of the days and nights he has lost, of the hunger and pain he has suffered, of the shame he still feels. For all of this, he wants revenge.

So when Morton, with his arms full of stolen weapons, said, "Let's burn it down," there was quick if not logical agreement. They felt in control again and they wanted to prove it. The Captain went to find a transport vehicle, and the other three began to destroy the camp. They used flame-throwers and big cans of oil to set the mine and the huts on fire.

"Burn!" Morton shouted.

"Burn!" Eddie shouted.

The mine exploded and black smoke rose from the entrance. Eddie watched and laughed, then moved down the path to the final, and biggest, hut. "This is the end," he said to himself. "The end." No more evil guards with bad teeth and bony faces. No more watery soup with insects floating in it. No more back-breaking work in a dirty coal mine. He didn't know what would happen to them next, but it couldn't be any worse than what they had lived through.

Eddie aimed the flame-thrower at the last hut and shot. The fire rose up within a minute and the walls turned into orange and yellow flames. In the distance, Eddie heard the sound of an engine. He hoped the Captain had found a vehicle for their escape. Then, suddenly, from the skies came the first sounds of bombing, the noise they had heard every night lately. It was even closer now, and Eddie realized that the burning huts were easy to see. If the planes were from their side, they might be rescued. He might be going home! He turned to the burning hut and ... "What was that?" He rubbed his eyes and looked again.

"What was that?"

Something ran across the door opening. The heat was extreme, and Eddie tried to protect his eyes with his free hand, but he had to look again. He wasn't sure, but he thought he had seen a small figure running inside the fire.

"Hey!" Eddie shouted, stepping forward. "HEY!" The roof of the hut began to fall, throwing burning pieces of the building everywhere. Eddie jumped back. Was it a shadow?

"EDDIE! NOW!" Morton was waving for Eddie to hurry.

Eddie was breathing hard. He pointed at the hut and shouted, "I think there's someone in there!"

Morton shook his head. He couldn't hear. Eddie turned and was almost certain he saw the figure again, there, inside the burning hut—a child. It made him think suddenly of his little cousins back at Ruby Park, waiting to get on the beautiful French carousel. He thought of the other rides and the children on the beach and Marguerite and her picture—everything he had tried not to think about for so many months.

"HEY! COME OUT!" he shouted, dropping the flame-thrower and moving closer. "I WON'T SHOO—"

A hand seized Eddie from behind. Eddie turned, ready to hit someone. It was Morton. "EDDIE! We have to go NOW!"

"No—no—wait—wait, I think there's someone in th—"

"There's nobody in there. NOW!" Morton screamed.

Eddie was desperate. He turned back toward the hut. He pushed Morton away and stepped forward, sure that someone innocent was inside there, burning to death in front of him. Then the whole roof fell and burning bits of it fell on his head.

In that one moment, Eddie felt the horror of war. He felt sick thinking about the guards, the murders, the bombs, the fires. He could not understand the reason for any of it. He just wanted to save something, a piece of Rabozzo, a piece of himself, and, even with the planes above him and the sound of bombs, he moved closer to the burning hut. He was so close to the building that his clothes caught fire.

"I'LL HELP YOU! COME OUT! I WON'T SHOO—"

A terrible pain hit his leg. He cried out and fell to the ground. Blood was pouring out of a bullet hole below his knee.

Bleeding and burning, for the first time in his life, Eddie felt ready to die. Then someone pulled him backward, rolled him in the dirt to put out the flames, and lifted him on to the transport vehicle. The others were around him, telling him to breathe, to stay calm. They were going to take care of him. His back was burned badly and he couldn't feel anything in his knee. His head was spinning, and he felt tired, so very tired.

♦

The Captain shook his head as Eddie remembered the scene at the burning hut.

"Do you remember how you got out of there?" he asked.

"Not really," Eddie said.

"It took two days. You were unconscious most of the time. You lost a lot of blood."

"We got away," Eddie said.

"Yeah, but the bullet really did some damage."

In fact, the bullet in Eddie's leg had cut through several nerves and badly broken a bone. After two surgeries, the doctors said Eddie would always walk with a limp, and it would get worse as he grew older. No more running or dancing. He learned many things as a soldier. He came home a different man.

"Did you know," the Captain said, "that I grew up in an army family? I took orders without question. Then I joined the army and started *giving* orders. When the war started, I could see the fear in the new soldiers' eyes. They thought that I could keep them alive, but I couldn't, of course. I took orders, too. But I thought I could at least keep my men together. In the middle of a big war, you look for a small idea to believe in. For me, that little idea was that no one gets left behind."

Eddie looked up. "That meant a lot," he said.

"I hope so," the Captain said. "Because I was the one who shot you."

Eddie looked at his bad leg. He felt the pain again. And he was terribly angry, wanting to hurt someone or something.

"Do it," the Captain whispered.

Eddie cried out and jumped at the Captain. The two men fell off the tree branch, to the ground below.

"WHY? WHY DID YOU RUIN MY LIFE? WHY?"

They were rolling on the muddy earth. Eddie was hitting the Captain in the face, but the Captain did not bleed. Eddie shook him by the collar and beat his head against the mud. The Captain was not hurt, and finally he rolled Eddie over.

"Because," he said calmly, "you would have died in that fire. I wasn't going to leave you behind. And it wasn't your time."

Eddie was breathing hard, "My ... time?"

"You refused to leave the burning hut, and we had about a minute to get out. Bombs were falling around us. Morton tried to make you come with him, but you were too strong to fight."

"But my leg! My ... leggggg! My *life!*" Eddie cried.

"I took your leg to save your life," the Captain said quietly.

"There was nobody in that hut," Eddie said. "What was I *thinking*? Why did I go in there?" His voice dropped to a whisper. "Why didn't I just *die?*"

"No one gets left behind, remember? Sometimes a soldier breaks down. Sometimes it's in the middle of a battle. A man drops his gun and his eyes go somewhere else. He can't fight any more. Usually he gets shot and dies. You broke down, but I could save you. I couldn't let you burn alive. I thought a leg would get better. We pulled you out of there, and the others took you to an army hospital."

Eddie thought for a minute. "The others? What about you? What do you mean, 'the *others*'?"

"Did you ever see me again?" the Captain asked.

Eddie thought about the night of their escape again. He could see himself lying in the back of the transport vehicle. The Captain was driving and Smitty and Morton were looking after him. They got to the top of a hill, and the Captain took his rifle and jumped out to check the path ahead, which curved into some trees. He ran about fifty yards beyond the curve.

The path was clear. The Captain waved to his men. A plane flew above them, and the Captain lifted his eyes to see if it was one of theirs. While he was looking toward heaven, he heard a small, sharp sound under his foot. The bomb, buried in the

40

ground, exploded immediately. It blew the Captain twenty feet into the air and split him into pieces. Bits of his burned flesh and bones flew over the muddy earth and landed in the trees.

♦

THE SECOND LESSON

"It's awful," Eddie said, closing his eyes. "God! I had no idea, sir. It's awful!"

The hills looked as they did on the day the Captain had died. This was the Captain's last resting place. No funeral. No prayers. Just pieces of his body and the muddy earth.

"You've been waiting here all this time?" Eddie whispered.

"Time," the Captain said, "is not what you think. Dying is not the end of everything. Our life on Earth is only the beginning." Eddie looked confused. "When you die, you enter a fresh new world, but you keep your yesterdays." The Captain lit a cigarette and continued, "Are you following this? I was never great at teaching."

"If you've been here since you died, that's twice as long as you lived. Right?" Eddie asked.

"I've been waiting for you," explained the Captain.

"That's what the Blue Man said."

"Like me, he was part of the story you need to know about your own life. After we tell you that part, we can move beyond here. This is what you need to know from me."

Eddie felt his back straighten.

"Sacrifice," the Captain said. "You made one. I made one. We all make them. But you were angry about yours. Sacrifice is a part of life. It's *supposed* to be. It's not something to regret. It's something to work toward. Little sacrifices. Big sacrifices. A mother works so her son can go to school. A daughter moves home to take care of her sick father. A man goes to war

41

... Rabozzo didn't die for nothing. He sacrificed his life for his country, and his family knew it, and his younger brother became a good soldier and a great man because his brother set an example for him.

"I didn't die for nothing, either. *I* stepped on that bomb, so the vehicle didn't drive over it and get all four of us killed."

"But you lost your life, and you were only about thirty."

"But when you sacrifice something valuable, you don't lose it. You pass it on to someone else. I shot you, and you lost something, but you also gained something. You just don't know it yet. I gained something, too."

"What?" asked Eddie.

"I was able to keep my promise. I didn't leave you behind."

The Captain held out his hand. "Forgive me about the leg?"

Eddie felt ashamed that he had had so much anger about his leg. He offered his hand.

The Captain took his hand and said, "That's what I've been waiting for."

"Captain, why did you meet me here? The Blue Man said you can choose where you want to wait."

The Captain smiled. "Because I died in battle. I was killed in these hills. When I left the world, I only knew about the army and war. I wanted to see the world *without* a war—before we started killing each other."

"But this *is* war," Eddie said as he looked around.

"To you. But our eyes are different," the Captain said. "We don't see the same things."

He lifted a hand and everything changed. The world again was a perfect place, untouched by war. Trees, flowers, and grass grew. The dark clouds parted and a yellow sun shone in a bright blue sky. Clear water surrounded the island.

Eddie looked up at his old commanding officer. The Captain's face was clean and his uniform looked new. He stood for a moment, enjoying the scene. Then he began to walk away from Eddie.

"Wait," Eddie shouted. "I need to know something. My death. At Ruby Park. Did I save that little girl? I felt her hands, but I can't remember ..."

The Captain scratched his head. He looked at Eddie sympathetically. "I can't tell you, soldier."

Eddie dropped his head.

"But someone can." Then he threw Eddie his helmet and dog tags. "Yours."

Eddie looked inside the helmet. He saw an old photo of a woman that made his heart ache again. When he looked up, the Captain was gone.

♦

MONDAY, 7:30 AM

The morning after the accident, Dominguez came to the maintenance shop early. Ruby Park was closed, but he came anyway, and he turned on the water at the sink. He thought he'd clean some of the ride parts. Then he shut off the water and listened. It seemed twice as quiet as it had a minute ago.

"What's happening?"

Willie was at the shop door. He was carrying a newspaper. The front-page story read: "Amusement Park Tragedy."

"I had a hard time sleeping," Dominguez said.

"Yeah." Willie sat down in one of the old chairs. "Me, too. When do you think they'll open the place again?"

Dominguez raised his shoulders. "Ask the police."

They sat quietly. They stared into space. They had another cup of coffee. It was Monday morning. They were waiting for the old man to come in and get the workday started.

Chapter 4
The Third Person Eddie Meets in Heaven

A sudden wind lifted Eddie, and the sky seemed to pull in close to him until he could feel it touching his skin like a blanket. Then it shot away and exploded into colors and stars—millions of stars, like salt spilled across a black cloth.

In a split second, Eddie was in the most wonderful mountains, with snow-covered tops, enormous rocky faces, and dark purple valleys. In one of the valleys, between two of the biggest mountains, was a large, black lake. The moon shone brightly in the water. In the distance, Eddie noticed some flashing lights and began walking in that direction, through ankle-deep snow which was neither cold nor wet.

"Where am I now?" Eddie thought. He examined his body and found that he was still very strong but his stomach was not as hard and tight as it had been when he was a soldier. He squeezed his injured knee and felt the old pain. He hadn't left it behind with the Captain. He was becoming the man he had been on Earth, with all his familiar problems. Why would heaven make you relive your own decay?

He walked toward the flashing lights and soon was surprised to find himself in front of a café, the kind he knew from his childhood. It was the shape of an old railroad car and had a curved red roof. A sign above it flashed the word "*EAT.*"

Eddie walked along the side of the café, looking through the windows. He could see a mixture of people: old and young, from the 1930s or the 1960s, black and white, with friends or alone. His eyes moved along to the last window and to a table in the right-hand corner. He froze.

He couldn't believe what he saw. "No," he heard himself whisper. He breathed deeply. His heart beat wildly. He looked again, then banged on the window.

"No!" Eddie shouted. "No! No!" He kept shouting until the word he wanted finally formed in his throat. He screamed the word so loudly that he thought his head would burst. But the man at the table did not look up, no matter how many times Eddie cried it, again and again:

"Dad! Dad! Dad!"

♦

Today is Eddie's Birthday

In the dark hallway of the army hospital, Eddie's mother, with Eddie's father, Joe, Marguerite, and Mickey Shea, walk toward Eddie's room with a birthday cake. As they enter Eddie's room, they begin singing, "Happy birthday to you, happy birthday to—"

Eddie is lying against a pillow. He has serious burns on his body, and he has already had surgery on his leg. He looks at these eager, happy faces and wants to run away.

Joe clears his throat. "Well, you look pretty good," he says. The others quickly agree. Good. Yes. Very good.

"Your mom got a cake," Marguerite whispers. She quietly leaves a little white bag of candy on Eddie's bedside table.

They all wish Eddie a happy birthday, and Eddie's mother cuts the cake. Only his father stands alone and silent.

Eddie catches his eye. His father looks down. Eddie uses all his strength to stop himself from crying.

♦

All parents damage their children. It cannot be helped, but there are different degrees of damage.

The damage done by Eddie's father was, at the beginning, the damage of neglect. As a baby, Eddie was rarely held by the man; as a child, he was mostly ignored. Eddie's mother was the loving parent, his father was there to punish him.

On Saturdays, Eddie's father used to take him to Ruby Park. Before the weekend arrived, Eddie imagined having fun on the carousel or the bumper cars, eating candy, and talking to his dad. But usually, after an hour or two, his father found a familiar face and said, "Watch the kid for me, will you?" Until his father returned late in the afternoon, often drunk, Eddie had to stay with one of the people who worked at the park.

Eddie remembered hours at the boardwalk, waiting for his father's attention, sitting on fences or on top of big tool boxes in the repair shop. Often he said, "I can help!" but the only job his dad gave him was climbing under the Ferris wheel in the morning, before the park opened, to collect the coins that had fallen from customers' pockets the night before.

At least four evenings a week, his father played cards. The table had money, bottles, cigarettes, and rules. Eddie's rule was simple: do not bother your father. Once he tried to stand next to his father and look at his cards, but the old man put down his cigarette and hit Eddie across the face with the back of his hand. "Stop breathing on me," he said. Eddie burst into tears and his mother pulled him to her waist, staring angrily at her husband. Eddie never got as close again.

Other nights, when the cards went bad and the bottles were empty, his father brought his anger into Eddie and Joe's bedroom. He threw their few toys at the wall. He took off his belt and beat them, screaming that they were wasting his money on worthless trash. Eddie used to pray for his mother to wake up, but even when she did, his father warned her to "stay out of it." This made it all even worse.

Violence. That was the second damage done in his childhood. Eddie could tell by the sound of his father's footsteps coming down the hall how bad the beating would be.

But through it all, despite it all, Eddie privately loved his dad, because sons love and admire their fathers through even the worst behavior. It is how they learn to be loyal. Before a boy can love God or a woman, he will love his father, even if this love cannot be explained.

And occasionally, his father let Eddie see that he was just a little bit proud of him. At the baseball field near Eddie's school, his father stood behind the fence, watching him play. If Eddie hit the ball out of the park, his father smiled, and when he did, Eddie raced around the bases. And these occasions kept the last bit of Eddie's love alive.

If he came home after a fight, his father always asked, "What happened to the other guy?" and Eddie said he gave him what he deserved. This, too, made his father smile. When Eddie attacked the kids who bothered his brother, Joe hid in his room, but his father said, "Forget about him. You're the strong one. Take care of your brother."

When Eddie was a teenager, he began working the same summer hours as his father at Ruby Park, rising before the sun, working at the park until it was dark. At first, he ran the simpler rides. In later years, he worked in the repair shop. Sometimes his father tested him with maintenance problems. He gave him a cracked wheel or a broken chain and said, "Fix it." And every time, after completing the job, Eddie placed the object in front of his father and said, "It's fixed."

Before dinner in the evenings, Eddie tried to clean his fingernails, but they always looked dirty, like his father's, from working on the park machinery. He caught his father watching him once and the old man smiled and said, "It shows you did a hard day's work." He held up his own dirty fingernails, before wrapping them around a glass of beer.

And then, one night, the speaking stopped completely. It was after the war and Eddie was out of the hospital and living at home again. His father had been drinking late at the local bar and found Eddie asleep on the couch when he came in.

Eddie's experiences in the war had changed him. He stayed inside, away from everyone, silently staring out the kitchen window, watching the carousel, rubbing his bad knee. His mother whispered that he "just needed time," but his father grew angrier with him each day. He didn't understand how desperate Eddie felt. He thought he was just weak and lazy.

"Get up!" he shouted now. He was drunk and shouted again, "Get up and get a job!"

Eddie tried to wake up.

The old man wasn't steady on his feet, but he came toward Eddie and pushed him. "Get up and get a job! Get up ... and ... GET A JOB!"

Eddie rose to his elbows.

"Get up and get a job! Get up and—"

"ENOUGH!" Eddie screamed, jumping to his feet, ignoring the burst of pain in his knee. He looked angrily at his father, whose face was just inches away. He could smell the bad breath of alcohol and cigarettes.

The old man pointed at Eddie's leg. "See? You ... aren't ... so ... hurt."

He started to swing at Eddie, but the younger man moved easily out of his way and caught his father's arm before he could hit him. The old man was completely surprised. This was the first time Eddie had ever defended himself, the first time he had done anything to try to stop his father's beatings. His father pulled away from Eddie. He stared at his son like a man watching a train pull away.

He never spoke to Eddie again.

This was the final damage that Eddie suffered. Silence. It marked their remaining years. His father was silent when Eddie moved into his own apartment, silent when Eddie took a job as a taxi driver, silent at Eddie's wedding, silent when Eddie came to visit his mother. She begged and cried, trying to get her husband to make peace with Eddie. But Eddie's father repeated, "That boy raised a hand to me." And that was the end of the conversation.

All parents damage their children. This was their life together. Neglect. Violence. Silence. And now, in a place beyond death, Eddie leaned against the wall of a café, troubled again by this man who denied him his love, a man who was ignoring him, even in heaven. His father. The damage done.

♦

"Don't be angry," a woman's voice said. "He can't hear you."

Eddie looked up in surprise. An old woman stood in front of him in the snow. Her face was thin and lined with age. She wore rose-colored lipstick, and her white hair was pulled back so tightly that you could see the pink skin beneath it. She wore old-fashioned glasses over narrow blue eyes.

Eddie could not remember ever seeing this woman in his past. Her handsome clothes and beautiful jewelry were from before his time. She stood very straight, holding an umbrella with both hands. Eddie guessed she'd been rich.

"Not always rich," she said with a smile. "I was raised like you were, in the poorer part of the city, forced to leave school when I was fourteen. My sisters and I were working girls. We gave every nickel back to the family—"

Eddie interrupted. He didn't want another story. "Why can't my father hear me?" he demanded.

She smiled. "Because his spirit—which is now very safe—is part of my heaven. But he is not really here. *You* are."

"Why does my father have to be safe for *you*?"

She paused and then said, "Come."

♦

Suddenly, they were at the bottom of the mountain. The café

was now just a tiny point of light in the distance.

"Beautiful, isn't it?" the old woman said. Eddie followed her eyes. There was something familiar about her—had he seen her photograph somewhere?

"Are you … my third person?"

"I certainly am," she said.

Eddie rubbed his head. *Who was this woman?* He had once hoped that he would meet the people he loved in heaven. At funerals he remembered the priest saying, "One day, we will all be together in Heaven." Where were the people that he *wanted* to meet again? Eddie felt more alone than ever.

"Can I see Earth?" he whispered.

She shook her head no.

"Can I talk to God?"

"You can always do that."

He hesitated before the next question. "Can I go back?"

She looked confused. "Back?"

"Yes, back," Eddie said. "To my life. To that last day. Is there something I can do? Can I promise to be good? Can I promise to go to church all the time? Something?"

"Why?" She seemed amused.

"Why? Why? Because this place makes no sense to me. Because I don't feel like I'm in heaven, if that's what I'm supposed to feel. I can't even remember my own death. I only remember two little hands—the little girl I was trying to save, I was pulling her out of the way. I think I was holding her hands and that's when I …"

"Died?" the old woman said, smiling.

"Died," he said, letting out a long breath. "Then I met you and the others—all this. Isn't a person supposed to have peace when they die?"

"You have peace," the old woman said, "when you make it with yourself."

"That's not how it works," Eddie said, shaking his head. He

50

couldn't tell her about his bad dreams, his lack of ambition after the war, the times he stood alone on the beach and watched as fish were pulled from the ocean in nets. He felt embarrassed because he saw that he was like those helpless creatures— trapped and beyond escape.

He didn't tell her that. Instead he said, "I don't want to offend you, lady, but I don't even know you."

"But I know you," she said.

"Really? How's that?"

"Well," she said, "if you have a moment, I shall tell you."

She sat down in a very lady-like manner and began to tell her story.

"I was a waitress at the Seahorse Grill, near the ocean where you grew up. Perhaps you remember it?"

"You?" Eddie said, almost laughing. "You were a waitress at the Seahorse? I used to have breakfast there years ago, before the building was destroyed. Good food. And not expensive."

"I loved my job as a waitress. I was an attractive girl in those days, and there were quite a few men who wanted to marry me. But no one was special enough. Then one day the finest-looking gentleman I had ever seen walked through the door. He was well-dressed and very confident. He was so polite when I served him, and I tried not to stare. When he paid his bill, he said his name was Emile, and he asked if he could take me out one evening.

"Emile was rich. He took me to places I had never been, bought me clothes, paid for meals, showed me a new, exciting life beyond the Seahorse Grill. He had earned his wealth in gas and steel, and didn't respect people who spent money that they didn't earn. I suppose he was attracted to a poor girl like me because we both enjoyed the simple things in life.

"We visited seaside hotels and amusement parks. We walked along the boardwalks and ate salty food. We went on the rides.

51

And we both loved the sea. One day, as we sat in the sand, watching the waves, he asked me to marry him.

"I was the happiest girl alive. I told him yes. We listened to the sounds of children playing happily in the ocean. Emile swore that he would build an amusement park for me, to capture our special moment—to keep us young forever.

"Emile kept his promise. He built the most wonderful place on Earth, with races and rides and boat trips and tiny railroads. There was a beautiful carousel from France and a Ferris wheel from Germany. And there were thousands of lights, so bright that at night you could see the park from a ship on the ocean.

"The entrance was finished last, and it was truly grand. Emile took me there and presented it to me. It was mine! Don't you remember the old entrance? Didn't you ever wonder about the name? Where you and your father worked?"

She touched her chest softly with her white-gloved fingers.

"I," she said, "am Ruby."

♦

Today is Eddie's Birthday

He is 33. He wakes suddenly from a deep sleep. He looks around at his bedroom, his wife. That dream. Will it ever stop?

The dream takes him back to the last night of war in the Philippines. He wanders through the flames, he hears the screams. He hears Smitty shouting for him. He opens his mouth, but no sound comes out. Then something hits his leg and he is pulled under the muddy earth. When he finally wakes up, he is left with a sense of darkness. A heavy gray cloud hangs over his day.

He doesn't talk to Marguerite about the dream, but she knows when something is bothering him. She holds him close and says, "What's wrong?" and he says, "Nothing, I'm just exhausted." How can he explain such sadness when she is supposed to make him happy? He knows only that something stepped in front of him, blocking his way, stealing his life. He gave up studying engineering, and he gave up the idea of traveling. He sat down in his life. And there he remained.

That night, after a tiring day of driving his taxi, he hears music coming from his apartment when he gets home. When he opens the door, Marguerite sings, "Happy birthday to you ..." in her soft, sweet voice. She looks beautiful in her best dress, with her hair and lips fixed specially for the occasion. Eddie tries to take a deep breath. He fights the darkness inside him. "Leave me alone," he tells it. "Let me feel this the way I should feel it."

Marguerite kisses him and gives him a birthday present and a small bag of their favorite candy from the boardwalk. But then there is a loud knock on the door.

"Eddie! Are you in there? Eddie?" The baker who lives below them is at the door. He looks worried.

"Eddie," he says. "Come downstairs. There's a phone call. I think something happened to your father."

♦

"I am Ruby."

It suddenly made sense to Eddie. He understood why the woman looked familiar. He had seen an old photograph, somewhere in the back of the repair shop.

"The old entrance ..." Eddie said.

The old lady smiled in satisfaction. Years ago, everyone recognized the Ruby Park entrance. It was famous all over the state for its extraordinary style and bright colors. Just beneath the big sign that said Ruby Park, under which all customers had to pass, was the painted face of a beautiful woman. *This* woman. Ruby.

"But that thing was destroyed a long time ago," Eddie said. "There was a big fire."

"Yes. A very big fire. It was the Fourth of July, the most

important day of the summer. Emile loved holidays. 'Good for business,' he always said. If the Fourth went well, the whole summer might go well. So Emile arranged for fireworks. He hired a marching band and extra workers, just for the weekend.

"But it was hot the night before the celebration, and a few of the temporary workers decided to sleep outside, behind the maintenance building. They lit a fire to cook their food on, and, of course, they began drinking.

"Later in the evening, they decided to light a few of the smaller fireworks. The wind blew some of them away from the men. Everything in those days was made of wood …

"The rest happened quickly. The fire spread to the rides, to the cafés, and to the animal cages. Someone came to our house to wake us. We looked out and saw the terrible orange flames. We heard the cries of the animals and the fire company's engines. The street was crowded with people.

"I begged Emile to stay in the house, but, of course, he had to try to save his years of work. He ran to the park and when the entrance with my picture and name caught fire, he lost all sense of where he was. He was trying to throw buckets of water when the entrance fell on him.

"Our lives changed forever that night. Emile was a risk-taker and had bought very little insurance on the park. He had to sell the property for much less than it was worth. Eventually, the new owner reopened Ruby Park, but it was no longer ours.

"Emile's spirit was as broken as his body. We moved to a small apartment outside the city where I could take care of him. I was sorry about only one thing."

She stopped.

"What were you sorry about?" Eddie asked.

"I was sorry that Emile had ever built Ruby Park."

The old woman was lost in thought. Eddie stared at the sky.

He thought about how many times he had wished for the same thing: a world without Ruby Park.

"I'm sorry about your husband," Eddie said, mostly because he didn't know what else to say.

"Thank you dear," the old woman said with a smile. "But we lived many years after the fire. We raised three children, but Emile was in and out of the hospital. I was a widow in my fifties and had to take care of myself and my family."

Eddie was thinking. "I don't understand. Did we ever ... meet? Did you ever come to Ruby Park after the fire?"

"No," she said. "I never wanted to see the park again. My idea of heaven was working in that busy café, when my days were simple, and where I met Emile and fell in love."

"So why am I here?" he said. "Your story and the fire happened before I was born."

"Things that happen before you are born still affect you," she said. "If I hadn't married Emile, you would not have spent your whole life working at Ruby Park."

"So you're here to tell me about working at Ruby Park?"

"No dear," Ruby answered softly. "I'm here to tell you why your father died."

♦

The phone call on Eddie's birthday was from his mother. His father had a terrible fever and was in the hospital.

"Eddie, I'm afraid," his mother said in a shaky voice. "Your father came home one night earlier this week at dawn. His clothes were wet and full of sand. One shoe was missing." Eddie bet that he was drunk. "He was coughing, and it got worse and worse. But he went to work as usual yesterday and the day before. But this afternoon, they brought him home from work. The doctor says he's seriously ill. Why didn't I do something sooner?"

55

"What were *you* supposed to do?" Eddie asked. He was sure it was all his father's fault because he had been drinking. But through the phone, he could hear his mother's crying.

Complications developed and his father's condition became worse and worse. Eddie helped at the park, working evenings after his taxi job, doing everything his father usually did, trying to protect the old man's job.

Finally, one night, to please his mother, Eddie visited the hospital. After years of silence from his father, Eddie found it difficult to think of anything to say. Then he did the only thing he could think of to do: He held up his hands and showed his father his dirty fingers. Eddie knew the old man would understand that he had been working at Ruby Park for him.

A few days later, when the news came that his father had died, Eddie felt the emptiest kind of anger, the kind that circles in its cage. Like all sons, Eddie had wanted a hero's end for his father, but he thought that there was nothing heroic about a drunken night on the beach.

The next day, he went to his parents' apartment and looked through drawers and cupboards, searching for a piece of his father. Finally, he found a pack of playing cards. He put it in his pocket.

The funeral was small and quick. In the weeks that followed, Eddie's mother lost her hold on reality. She thought that she was still living with her husband. She chatted to him about her day. She shouted at him to turn down the radio. She cooked enough food for two. She packed a lunch for him to take to work every day.

One night, Eddie tried to put some dishes into the cupboard for her. "Leave them," his mother said. "Your father will put them away."

Eddie put a hand on her shoulder.

"Ma," he said, softly. "Dad's gone."

"Gone where?"

The next day, Eddie left his job with the taxi firm. Two weeks later, he and Marguerite moved back into the apartment where Eddie had grown up, and where you could see the carousel from the kitchen window. Eddie accepted a job that would let him keep an eye on his mother: maintenance man at Ruby Park. Eddie never said this—not to his wife, not to his mother, not to anyone—but he cursed his father for dying and trapping him in the life he had been trying to escape; a life, as he heard the old man laughing from the grave, that it seemed was now good enough for him.

♦

THE THIRD LESSON

"Was the park so bad?" the old woman asked.

"It wasn't my choice," Eddie said. "My mother needed help. One thing led to another. Years passed. I never left. I never lived anywhere else. Never made any real money. You know how it is—you get used to something, people depend on you, one day you wake up and you can't tell Tuesday from Thursday. You're doing the same boring stuff, you're Mr. Maintenance, just like …"

"Your father?"

Eddie said nothing.

"He pushed you hard," the old woman said.

Eddie looked at the floor. "Yeah. So?"

"Maybe you made things difficult for him, too."

"I doubt it. Do you know how often he hit me? Do you know the last time he spoke to me?"

"Yes, he told you to get a job. And you stopped feeling sorry for yourself and found work after that."

"Listen," Eddie said angrily. "You didn't know the guy."

"That's true, but I have something to show you."

Ruby drew a circle in the snow with the point of her umbrella and created a hole. Eddie looked down the hole and observed a moment from years ago in the old apartment. He could see everything—front and back, above and below.

This is what he saw:

His mother was sitting at the kitchen table, looking sympathetic. His father's friend Mickey Shea was sitting across from her. He looked awful. His clothes were wet, and he kept rubbing his forehead with his hands. He began to cry. Eddie's mother brought him a glass of water. Then she excused herself, walked into the bedroom, and shut the door. She took off her shoes and her housedress. She reached for a blouse and skirt.

Eddie could see all of the rooms, but he couldn't hear anything that his mother and Mickey said to each other. In the kitchen, Mickey took a bottle of alcohol from his jacket and took a long drink. Then, he walked slowly and unsteadily to the bedroom and opened the door.

Eddie saw his mother, half dressed, turn in surprise. She pulled a sweater around her as Mickey came closer. He pushed Eddie's mother against the wall and tried to pull the sweater off her shoulders. She struggled, trying to move away, then shouted and pushed Mickey's chest. He was bigger and stronger, and he buried his unshaven face below her cheek, wiping his tears on her neck.

Then the front door opened, and Eddie's father stood there, wet from rain, with his tool belt around his waist. He heard his wife's cries and ran into the bedroom. When he saw Mickey pressing against his wife, he shouted and raised his hammer. Mickey put his hands over his head and rushed to the door, knocking Eddie's father out of the way. Eddie's mother was crying, tears streamed down her cheeks. Her husband shook her violently. Her sweater fell. They were both screaming. Then Eddie's father left the

58

apartment, breaking a lamp with the hammer on his way out. He raced down the steps and ran off into the rainy night.

Now Eddie could see a storm at the farthest edge of Ruby Park. The sky was black and rain came down in great sheets. Mickey Shea walked drunkenly toward the end of the boardwalk. Then, possibly on purpose, he fell into the sea.

Eddie's father appeared moments later, still holding the hammer. He searched the waters. The wind blew the rain sideways. He was wet to the skin. Then he saw something in the waves. He stopped, pulled off the tool belt, removed his shoes and jumped into the wild ocean.

Mickey was struggling against the rolling water, half unconscious, a yellow liquid coming from his mouth. Eddie's father swam to him. Mickey tried to hit him. Eddie's father struck back. The sky lit up with a flash of lightning.

Mickey coughed hard as Eddie's father took his arm and pulled it over his shoulder. He went under, came up again, then held Mickey's body tightly against his side and pointed them toward shore. He kicked. They moved forward. A wave swept them back. Then forward again. Eddie's father kicked harder, trying desperately to see where the beach was.

Then a wave suddenly pushed them forward and dropped them onto the sand. Eddie's father rolled out from under Mickey and held him so that the enormous wave would not sweep him back into the sea. When the waves calmed down a bit, Eddie's father fell on the shore, his mouth open, filling with wet sand.

♦

The scene changed and Eddie was looking at Ruby again. He felt exhausted, as if he had been in that ocean himself.

"What was my father *doing*?" Eddie whispered.

"Saving a friend," Ruby said.

Eddie stared at her. "What kind of friend was he? If I'd

known what he did, I'd have let his worthless soul drown."

"Your father thought about that, too," the old woman said. "He had chased Mickey to hurt him, maybe even kill him. But in the end, he couldn't. He knew who Mickey was. He knew he drank too much. He knew he made mistakes, lots of them.

"But it was because of Mickey that your dad got his job at Ruby Park. And when you were born, Mickey lent your parents money, to help with the cost of having a new baby. Your father was serious about old friendships—"

"Wait a minute!" shouted Eddie. "Did you see what that drunk was doing with my mother?"

"I did," the old woman said sadly. "It was wrong. But we don't always understand the whole picture. Mickey had been fired that afternoon. He'd been drunk and hadn't shown up at work. His employers told him it had happened too many times. Mickey began drinking more. By the time he reached your apartment, he was very drunk. He was begging for help. He wanted his job back. Your father was working late, and your mother was going to take Mickey to him.

"Mickey was rough, but he was not evil. When he got to the apartment, he felt lost. He wasn't thinking. His actions were the actions of a desperate, lonely man. At first, your father wasn't thinking either. He wanted to kill Mickey, but then he wanted to keep his friend alive.

"That was how your father became so sick, of course. He lay there on the beach for hours, without the strength to struggle home. You father was already fifty-six—not a young man. The experience made him weak, and then he died."

"Because of Mickey?" Eddie said.

"Because he was loyal to a friend," she said.

"People don't die because they are loyal."

"They don't?" she smiled. "Are we not loyal to religion? To government? To our country? Don't we die for those things?"

Eddie didn't know what to say.

"Better," she said, "to be loyal to one another."

After several minutes, Eddie asked, "What happened to Mickey Shea?"

"He died alone, a few years later," the old woman said. "Too much drink. He never forgave himself for what happened."

"But my father—" Eddie said, rubbing his forehead. "He never said anything."

"He didn't say anything about that night to anyone. He was ashamed for your mother, for Mickey, for himself. In the hospital, he stopped speaking completely. Silence was his escape, but his thoughts still bothered him. One night, his breathing slowed and his eyes closed and he could not be woken up. After that, your mother stayed by his bedside. Days and nights. She kept repeating, 'Why didn't I do something? Why didn't I do something ...'

"Finally, one night, the doctor persuaded her to go home to sleep. Early the next morning, a nurse found your father hanging halfway out the window."

"Wait," Eddie said. His eyes narrowed. "The window?"

"Yes," Ruby said, "sometime during the night, your father woke up. He got out of bed and struggled to get to the window and open it. Softly, he called your mother's name, and he called yours, too, and your brother Joe's. And he called for Mickey. At that moment, it seemed, his heart was letting go of all the guilt and regret. Maybe he felt the light of death approaching. Maybe he only knew you were all out there somewhere. But the cold, wet, windy weather was too much for him. He was dead before dawn. The nurses who found him dragged the body back to his bed. They were frightened for their jobs, so they said he had died in his sleep."

Eddie was speechless. The rough old working man, trying to climb out a window. What was he thinking? Which was worse: an unexplained life or an unexplained death?

"How do you know all this?" Eddie asked Ruby.

"Your father couldn't afford a private hospital room. Neither could the man on the other side of the curtain." She paused. "Emile. My husband."

Eddie lifted his eyes. Suddenly, he had solved a puzzle.

"Then you *saw* my father and my mother."

"Yes. I heard your mother crying softly on those lonely nights. We never spoke. But after your father's death, I asked about your family. When I learned that your father had worked at Ruby Park, I felt a stinging pain, like I had lost someone from my own family. The park was named for me, but it had ruined my life. Again, I was sorry that it had ever been built.

"That wish followed me to heaven." She pointed to the light in the distance. "The café. It's there because I wanted to return to my younger years—a safe, simple life. I wanted everyone who had ever suffered at Ruby Park—every accident, every fire, every fight, every fall—to be whole and safe. I wanted all of them, like I wanted my Emile, to be warm, well fed, happy—and far from the sea."

Eddie stood up. He could not stop thinking about his father. "I hated him," he whispered. "He was cruel to me when I was a kid. And he was worse when I got older."

Ruby stepped toward him. "Edward," she said softly. It was the first time she had called him by name. "Learn this from me. Anger can poison you. It eats you from inside. We think that hate is a weapon against our enemies. But hatred is a curved blade. And the harm we do, we do to ourselves.

"Forgive, Edward. Forgive. Do you remember how light, how free you felt when you first arrived in heaven?"

Eddie did. *Where is my pain?*

"That's because no one is born with anger. And when we die, the soul is freed of it. But now, here, to move on, you must understand why you felt what you did. You don't need to feel anger now."

She touched his hand. "You need to forgive your father."

Eddie thought about the years that followed his father's funeral. For him, they were years full of regrets. His father's death and his mother's poor health kept him at Ruby Park, in the dirty, boring job that his father had left behind. Eddie had a picture in his head of lost possibilities. He blamed his father for his loss of freedom, his loss of career, his loss of hope.

"When he died," Eddie said, "he took part of me with him. I was stuck after that."

"Your father was not the reason you never left the park."

Eddie looked up at the old woman. "Then what was?"

"There are still two people for you to meet," she said as she walked away.

♦

Ruby was gone. Eddie was back on top of the mountain, outside the café, standing in the snow.

When he realized that Ruby was not coming back, Eddie slowly pulled the café door open. He smelled freshly cooked food and heard the noise of customers eating, drinking, and talking. Walking to the corner table, to the ghost of his father, Eddie thought about the old man hanging out that hospital window, dying alone in the middle of the night.

"Dad?" Eddie whispered.

His father could not hear him. Eddie went closer. "Dad. I know what happened now." Eddie looked at his father's tired eyes, his bent nose, the rough hands and strong shoulders of a working man.

"I was angry with you, Dad. I hated you. You beat me. You shut me out. I didn't understand—I still don't. Why did you do it? Why?" Eddie's chest was shaking. Tears filled his eyes.

"I didn't know what happened in your life. OK? I didn't *know* you. But you're my father. Can we let the past go?"

Now he was screaming. "OK? CAN YOU HEAR ME?"

Then softer: "Can you hear me? Dad?" He looked at his father's dirty hands. He whispered the familiar words that would please the old man: "It's fixed."

Eddie looked up and saw Ruby standing at the counter, looking young and beautiful. She smiled at Eddie, and then she went to the door, opened it, and disappeared into the night sky.

♦

THURSDAY, 11 AM

Who was going to pay for Eddie's funeral? He had no relatives. He hadn't left any instructions. His uniform, his socks and heavy shoes, his old cap, his wedding ring, his cigarettes, and balloons were in a package, waiting for someone to claim them.

In the end, Mr Bullock, the park owner, used the money from Eddie's last pay-check to pay for a cheap funeral. The closest church to Ruby Park was chosen so people could get back to work quickly.

Before the service, the priest asked Dominguez, dressed in his good jeans and a jacket, to step into his office. "Could you share some of your friend's special qualities with us?"

Dominguez swallowed. He wasn't comfortable with priests. He spoke as softly as he thought he should in such a situation.

"Eddie," he finally said, "really loved his wife. Of course, I never met her."

Chapter 5
The Fourth Person Eddie Meets in Heaven

Now Eddie found himself in a small, round, empty room. There was no furniture and there were no windows in the room, but there was a row of doors.

There are still two people for you to meet, Ruby had said. And then what?

Eddie limped over to one of the doors and pushed it open. Suddenly, he was outside, in the backyard of a home he had never seen, in a country he did not recognize, in the middle of a wedding celebration. The yard was decorated with red flowers, and the new wife, young and pretty, was the center of attention. The guests cheered as her handsome husband presented her with a ring from the end of his sword. Eddie could not understand the language that they were speaking. German? Swedish?

Eddie coughed. The group looked up. People smiled, but no one spoke. Eddie backed through the door and entered a different wedding scene. This time he was indoors in a large hall, where the people looked Spanish. The new wife was dancing from one partner to the next, and each guest handed her a small sack of coins.

Eddie coughed again—he couldn't help it—and each time he coughed, he found himself in the middle of another wedding celebration. In an African scene, he watched families pour wine on the ground, and the happy couple held hands and jumped over a stick. In China, fireworks were lit and the guests cheered loudly. In France—maybe—he saw the new husband and wife drink from a cup with two handles.

At each wedding party, everyone looked happy, but no one spoke directly to him. He thought this was like the weddings he had gone to on Earth. He couldn't join in the dancing because of his bad leg, and after Marguerite died, he had to go everywhere alone. Usually, on these occasions, he stood around in the parking lot, smoking a cigarette, waiting for time to pass. He was considered an "old man," without a partner, and no one expected him to join in the fun.

As he moved from one wedding reception to the next, Eddie wondered about the connection to *his* life. He pushed open another door and found himself at a charming wedding reception in, he thought, an Italian village. He found a place against a wall and watched as the new couple danced their first dance as husband and wife. He looked around at the crowd and noticed a young woman in a light purple dress. She moved among the guests with a basket of candy.

"*Per l'amaro e il dolce?*" she said, offering her sweets.

At the sound of her voice, Eddie's whole body shook. Something told him to run, but something else froze his feet to the ground. The beautiful young woman came toward him.

"*Per l'amaro e il dolce?*" she said, smiling, holding out the candy. "For the bitter and the sweet?"

Eddie's heart almost burst. He dropped to his knees.

"Marguerite ..." he whispered.

"For the bitter and the sweet," she said quietly.

◆

Today is Eddie's Birthday

Eddie and his brother Joe are sitting in the maintenance shop at Ruby Park. Joe has come to wish Eddie a happy birthday and to show Eddie his new car. Joe is a salesman, making three times as much money as Eddie makes.

"*Hello? Anybody in there?*"

Marguerite is at the door, holding a wheel of orange tickets. She's wearing a Ruby Park uniform for her job in the ticket office this summer. Eddie feels embarrassed for her in front of his successful brother.

"*Hello, Joe. Can I borrow Eddie for just a minute, please?*"

Eddie stands up slowly and follows his wife out the door.

"*HAP-PY BIRTH-DAY, MR. ED-DIE!*" *a group of children scream as they stand outside in the sunshine.*

Marguerite shouts, "OK, kids, put the candles on the cake!"

As the children race around, Marguerite whispers to Eddie, "I promised you'd blow out all thirty-eight candles at once."

Marguerite is always in a good mood around children, and it hurts Eddie to remember that she can't have any of her own. One doctor said she was too nervous. Another said she was too old. Eventually, they ran out of money for doctors.

For about a year, Marguerite has been talking about adoption. She went to the library. She brought home information. Eddie said he'd think about it.

When the candles are lit, Marguerite says, "Wait! I've got Charlene's camera. I want to take a picture."

Marguerite takes a photograph of Eddie blowing out his candles with the children squeezing around him. "Blow them all out, OK?" one of the kids shouts.

"I will," Eddie says, looking at his wife.

◆

Eddie stared at the young Marguerite.

"It's not you," he said. "It can't be you."

She offered her hand. Eddie reached for it quickly, and when their fingers met he had the most wonderful, the gentlest, the warmest feeling in the world. Marguerite knelt beside him.

"It *is* me," she whispered.

"It's not you, it's not you, it's not you," Eddie whispered, as he dropped his head onto her shoulder and, for the first time since his death, began to cry.

◆

Eddie and Marguerite had gotten married on Christmas Eve, on the second floor of a dark Chinese restaurant called Sammy Hong's. Eddie spent the cash he had left from the army on the reception: roast chicken, Chinese vegetables, cheap wine and a man with a guitar. The chairs for the ceremony were needed for the dinner, so after the wedding, the guests carried them down to the restaurant for the reception.

After the meal, Eddie and Marguerite left through the front door. A few of the guests threw rice from the kitchen. It was cold and raining lightly. Marguerite wore her wedding dress beneath a thick pink sweater. Eddie wore his white suit coat over a shirt and a black necktie that felt too tight. They were happy, holding hands and walking the few blocks home through the empty streets.

♦

People say they "find" love. They refer to it like an object hidden under a rock. But love takes many forms, and it is never the same for anyone else. Each person finds his or her own special love. Eddie found his with Marguerite—a grateful love, a deep but quiet love. He knew that no other love could ever take the place of his love for his wife. After she died, his days seemed dry and lifeless. He put his heart to sleep.

Now, here she was again, as young as the day they were married in Sammy Hong's Chinese restaurant.

"Walk with me," she said.

Eddie could only stare. She was exactly as he remembered— more beautiful, really, because his final memories of her had been of an older, suffering woman. He stood beside her, silent, until her dark eyes narrowed and she smiled playfully.

"Eddie." She almost laughed. "Have you forgotten how I used to look?"

Eddie swallowed. "I could never forget that."

She pointed at the village and the dancing guests. "I chose to have weddings behind every door. They are such magical occasions all around the world. Two people's lives full of possibilities. Two people who truly believe their love will last a life-time." She smiled. "Do you think we had that?"

Eddie didn't know how to answer. "We had a guitar player," he said.

They walked away from the wedding reception and down a

country path. Eddie wanted to tell her everything he had seen, everything that had happened since she died. He also wanted to know about her time in heaven.

"Did you meet five people?" he asked.

"Yes, just like you."

"And did they explain everything? Did it make a difference?" Eddie was anxious to know her story.

She smiled. "They made all the difference." She touched his chin. "And then I waited for you."

"Do you know about my life? My life after you died?"

"I know most things. And the most important thing I know is that you loved me dearly. But I don't know how *you* died."

Eddie told her about the new rides at Ruby Park, especially about Freddy's Free Fall. And about his last day on Earth. He explained that he was not sure what had happened to the little girl he tried to save. Finally, Eddie said, "I haven't talked as much as this since I got here."

Marguerite smiled, and Eddie's eyes filled with tears. He couldn't believe that he was really here, really talking to his wife. A sadness rose up in his heart, and he could only think of what he had lost. He was looking at his young wife, his dead wife, his only wife, and he didn't want to look any more.

"Marguerite," he whispered. "I'm so sorry, I'm so sorry. I can't say. I can't say. I can't say."

He dropped his head into his hands and he said it anyway. He said what everyone says: "I missed you so much."

♦

Today is Eddie's Birthday

Eddie and his old friend Noel left work early and went to the races. Their plan was to bet on Eddie's birthday number, 39, in the Daily Double. At their feet are empty paper cups of beer and a carpet of used tickets.

69

Eddie won the first race of the day. He put half of the money he had won on the second race and won that, too. It was the first time anything like that had ever happened to him. That gave him $209. Then he lost twice on smaller bets, but decided to put everything he had left on a horse to win in the sixth race.

"Just think, if you win," Noel says, "you'll have all that cash for the kid."

The bell rings. The horses are running. Eddie has bet on a horse named Jersey Finch. But he's thinking about what Noel has said. Eddie and Marguerite are planning to adopt a child. They need that money. Why did he risk it on a horse?

The crowd is on their feet. The horses are near the finish line. Everyone is cheering. Noel is shouting. Eddie squeezes his ticket. He is more nervous than he wants to be. His skin feels cold. One horse pulls ahead of the pack.

Jersey Finch! Now Eddie has almost $800.

"I'm going to call home," he says.

"You'll ruin your luck if you tell someone," warns Noel.

"That's crazy. I'm calling her. It'll make her happy."

"It won't make her happy," Noel says.

Noel is right. Marguerite is not happy. She tells Eddie to come home. He tells her to stop telling him what to do.

"We have a baby coming," she shouts. "You can't keep behaving like this."

Eddie hangs up the phone and goes to the window to pick another horse. He takes the money from his pocket and bets all of it on a horse in the next race.

At home, Marguerite feels bad about shouting at Eddie on his birthday. She wants to apologize and decides to drive to the race course and find him. She also wants to tell him to stop betting. She knows from other evenings that Noel will want to stay until closing time. She drives down Lester Street, where she will have to drive under a bridge to get to the race course.

But on this night, there are two drunken teenagers on the bridge.

*They stole two bottles of alcohol and several packs of cigarettes from a
local supermarket and have drunk the alcohol and smoked a lot of the
cigarettes. Now one of them is holding one of the empty bottles over the
side of the bridge.*

"Dare me?" the boy asks his friend.

"Yeah, I dare you," says the second boy.

*The first boy lets the bottle drop. The boys watch it miss a car and
break into pieces on the busy road.*

*"Drop yours now!" the first boy shouts at his friend. "Don't be a
coward!" The second boy holds out his bottle and laughs. He swings
the bottle from side to side and then lets it fly.*

*Forty feet below, Marguerite never thinks to look up, never thinks
that anything might drop out of the sky. She is thinking about Eddie
when a heavy bottle hits her car window, making her lose control of
the vehicle. The car hits the side of the bridge. Marguerite is thrown
against the door. Her arm is broken. Her head crashes against the front
window. Her body is badly damaged. She is unconscious when the
ambulance arrives. She does not hear two teenagers running across the
bridge and into the night.*

◆

The accident on Lester Street put Marguerite in the hospital.
She had to stay in bed for six months. Because she was so
badly injured, the child they were expecting to adopt went to
another couple. Neither she nor Eddie ever mentioned blame,
but Marguerite went quiet for a long time. Eddie lost himself
in work, where things were always changing and newer rides
were always being brought in.

But the shadow of blame took a place at their table, and
they ate in its presence. When they spoke, they spoke of small,
unimportant things. Their love was still there, but deeply
hidden for a long time. Eddie never bet on the horses again.
He lost contact with Noel.

In time, husband and wife began talking again, and one night, Eddie even spoke about adopting. Marguerite rubbed her forehead and said, "We're too old now."

The years passed. And although a child never came, their love grew strong again and filled the space they had been saving for the baby. In the mornings, she made him toast and coffee, and he dropped her at her cleaning job and then drove back to Ruby Park. Sometimes in the afternoon, she finished early and walked along the boardwalk with him. They shared a little bag of their favorite candy, and Eddie told her about his day and the problems with the machines. They were both in their forties now and happy again in each other's company.

Three years later, when Marguerite was forty-seven years old, she was preparing a roast chicken in the kitchen of their apartment, the one they had kept after Eddie's mother died because Marguerite said it reminded her of when they were teenagers, and she liked to look at the old carousel from the kitchen window. Suddenly, without warning, the fingers of her right hand stretched open and she could not close them. The chicken fell into the sink. She had a terrible pain in her arm. Her breathing became very quick and shallow.

"Eddie?" she called, but by the time he arrived, she was unconscious on the kitchen floor.

It was, the hospital doctors said, a tumor on the brain, and the cure would be difficult and often painful.

In her final days, when there was nothing more that the medical profession could do for her, her doctors said only, "Rest. Relax." She told them that she wanted to go home.

Eddie helped her up the stairs and hung her coat as she looked around the apartment. He made a simple dinner and served it to Marguerite and several friends from Ruby Park. Everyone was happy to see her, but they knew this was a party to say "goodbye," not "welcome home."

Two days later, she woke up before dawn with a scream. Eddie rushed her to the hospital. They parked in the lot and Eddie turned off the engine. It was suddenly too quiet. The only thing Eddie could think about was holding on to Marguerite. He couldn't lose her.

He opened the door and helped her get out. She pulled her coat more tightly around her, like a freezing child. Her hair blew across her face. She smelled the air and lifted her eyes toward Ruby Park.

"Look, Eddie, you can see it from here," she said.

"The Ferris wheel?" he said.

She looked away. "Home."

♦

Together with Marguerite again, in heaven, Eddie wanted only one thing: time—more and more time—and they received it. They spent every moment together. They talked about everything. Eddie told her about his brother Joe's death from a heart attack. She asked if he had kept the old apartment. He told her about the other three people he had met in heaven, and how he had made things right with his father. This pleased her, and Eddie felt an old, warm feeling he had missed for years—the simple act of making his wife happy.

They talked about Eddie's life at Ruby Park, and about how so many things there had changed.

"I'm sorry I never worked anywhere else," he told her. "I'm sorry I never got us out of there. My dad. My leg. I always felt worthless after the war."

Marguerite looked at the sad look on his face and asked, "What happened during the war?"

Soldiers, in Eddie's day, did what they had to do and didn't speak of it after they came home. He thought about the men he'd killed. He thought about the cruel guards. He thought about the blood on his hands. He wondered if he'd ever be forgiven.

"I lost myself," he whispered. They were both silent.

At times, there in heaven, the two of them lay down together. But they did not sleep. Instead, Eddie held her shoulders and smelled her hair. At one point, he asked his wife if God knew he was here. She smiled and said, "Of course," even when Eddie admitted that some of his life he'd spent hiding from God, and the rest of the time he thought he was unnoticed.

♦

THE FOURTH LESSON

Finally, after many conversations, Marguerite walked Eddie through another door. They were back inside the small, round room.

She sat on the wooden chair. "Each young woman waits here for her new life to begin. This is the moment when you think about what you're doing. Who you're choosing. Who you will love for the rest of your life. If it's right, Eddie, this can be such a wonderful moment."

She turned to him. "You had to live without love for many years, didn't you? You felt that I had left you too soon."

"You *did* leave too soon," he said.

"You were angry with me, weren't you?"

"No!" he shouted. "Well … yes. You weren't old enough to die. You were only forty-seven. You were the best person any of us knew, and you died, and you lost everything. And I lost everything. I lost the only woman I ever loved."

She took his hands. "No, you didn't. I was right here. And you loved me anyway. Lost love is still love, Eddie. It takes a different form, that's all. Memory. Memory becomes your partner. You hold it. You dance with it. Life has to end," she said. "Love doesn't."

"I never wanted anyone else," he said quietly. "I was still in love with you."

"I know," she smiled. "I felt it."

"Here?"

"Even here. That's how strong lost love can be."

Marguerite stood and opened a door. Eddie followed her into a dark room, with a few rows of restaurant chairs, and a guitar player sitting in the corner.

"I was saving this one," she said.

She held out her arms. And for the first time in heaven, Eddie forgot about his leg and ignored all the ugly associations he had made about dance and music and weddings, realizing now that they were really about loneliness.

He smiled and put a hand behind his wife's waist.

"Can I ask you something?" he said.

"Yes."

"Why do you look the way you looked the day I married you?"

"I thought you'd like it that way."

He thought for a moment. "Can you change it? Can you look like you did at the end?"

She dropped her arms. "I wasn't so pretty at the end."

Eddie shook his head. For him, that certainly wasn't true.

Marguerite took a moment, then came again into his arms. The guitar man played the familiar notes. She and Eddie began to move together, slowly, in the remembered steps that a husband shares only with his wife.

Marguerite sang softly in Eddie's ear: "You made me love you ..." Their song.

When Eddie moved his head back, she was forty-seven again, with a few lines beside her eyes, thinner hair, looser skin beneath her chin. She smiled and he smiled, and she was, to him, as beautiful as ever. He closed his eyes and said for the first time what he'd been feeling from the moment he saw her again: "I don't want to go on. I want to stay here."

When he opened his eyes, his arms still held her shape, but she was gone, and everything else was gone, too.

♦

FRIDAY, 3:15 PM

Dominguez went to Eddie's apartment with the lawyer. They left the old elevator and turned toward apartment 6B. The hallway hadn't changed in more than fifty years, and it smelled of cooking—bacon and fried potatoes. They had to clear out Eddie's home before next Wednesday, in time for someone new to move in.

"Look at this," Dominguez said, as he opened the door and entered the kitchen. "Pretty neat for an old guy." Everything was clean and in its place.

"Insurance papers? Bank statements? Any jewelry?" the lawyer asked. He looked at his watch. If this didn't take too much time, he could be home for dinner.

Dominguez thought of Eddie wearing jewelry and almost laughed. He realized how strange it was at the park without the old man. Now no one was there giving orders, watching everything like a protective mother hen.

"You know, I was only here once. I really only knew Eddie through work," Dominguez explained. He leaned on the table and noticed that he could see the old French carousel through Eddie's kitchen window.

In the bedroom chest of drawers, the lawyer found neatly arranged underwear and an old leather box, but no important papers. Just a thin black necktie, a Chinese restaurant menu, an old pack of cards, a letter with an army medal, and an old photograph of a man in a Ruby Park uniform beside a birthday cake, surrounded by children.

"Hey, is this what you need?" shouted Dominguez from the kitchen. He had found a pile of envelopes in a drawer.

The lawyer looked through them quickly and, seeing letters from Eddie's bank, said, "This is all we need." Silently, he congratulated himself on his own good job, his money in the bank, and his solid plans for the future. Much better, he thought, than leaving nothing more than a clean kitchen.

Chapter 6
The Fifth Person Eddie Meets in Heaven

White. There was only white now. No earth, no sky, nothing to separate the two. Only a pure white, as silent as the deepest snow at the quietest sunrise.

White was all Eddie saw. All he heard was his own heavy breathing, followed by the sound of that breathing, repeated somewhere beyond him. He took another breath and heard a louder breath taken somewhere else. He breathed out, and another distant breath was let out.

Eddie squeezed his eyes shut. Silence is worse when you know it won't be broken, and Eddie knew. His wife was gone. He wanted her desperately—one more minute, half a minute, five more seconds—but there was no way to reach or call or wave or even look at her picture. He felt like a man who had fallen down a flight of stairs and lay helpless at the bottom. He had no wish to move. He hung lifeless in space, like a fish on a hook, with his soul bleeding out of him. Maybe he had hung there for a day or a month. Maybe it was for a century.

Then a small, mysterious noise brought him to consciousness again. His eyes lifted heavily. He had already been to four places in heaven and met four people, and while each meeting had been confusing on his arrival, he sensed that this was something completely different.

He heard the noise again, louder now, and he automatically prepared to defend himself. His hand squeezed his cane tightly. He looked down at his old body. His arms and legs were marked with signs of decay: lines, spots, loose flesh. In human terms, his body was near its end.

Now he heard the sound again. High, irregular cries and screams. Eddie was reminded of the frightening dreams he used to have, and he shook with the memory of them. The village, the fire, Smitty, and this awful noise. He tried to speak, but the same noise came out of his own throat.

The noise refused to stop, like an alarm that goes off in the night. Then Eddie shouted into the terrible white all around him: "What is it? *What do you want?*"

Suddenly, everything changed again. The awful noise turned into the sound of a running river, and Eddie could see the sun in the sky. Ground appeared beneath his feet. His cane touched something solid. From high up on the side of a hill, he looked down and saw, in the river, the reason for that mysterious noise. He relaxed immediately. The awful screaming, whistling noise was only the sound of children's voices, thousands of them playing in the river and laughing and shouting innocently.

"Was this what I dreamed about?" he thought. "All this time? Why?"

He studied the small bodies, some jumping, some swimming, some carrying buckets while others rolled in the high grass. He noticed a certain calmness to it all—no rough, violent play, which you usually saw with a big group of kids. He noticed something else. There were no adults. Not even teenagers. These were all small children, with skin the color of dark wood, and they were taking care of themselves.

78

And then Eddie noticed a big, white rock. A thin young girl stood on it, apart from the other children, facing in his direction. She signaled to him with her hands. He hesitated. She smiled and waved, and then pointed directly at him.

Eddie tried to walk down the hill. He slipped—his bad knee couldn't hold him. But before he hit the earth, he felt a sudden burst of wind at his back, and he was pushed forward and stood straight on his feet. And there he was, standing in front of the little girl.

◆

Today is Eddie's Birthday

He is fifty-one. A Saturday. It is his first birthday without Marguerite. He makes a cup of coffee and eats two pieces of toast with jelly. In the years after his wife's accident, Eddie refused to have any birthday celebrations, saying, "Why do I have to be reminded of that day?" But Marguerite had always made his birthdays special. She made a cake. She invited friends. She always gave him a bag of their favorite candy from the boardwalk. "You can't give away your birthday," she liked to say.

Now that she's gone, Eddie tries to forget about his birthday. He works late at the park. At home, he watches television and goes to bed early. No cake. No guests. His days are all the same now: dull and pale.

He is sixty-eight. Another Saturday. He spreads his pills on the counter in the kitchen. The telephone rings. Joe, his brother, is calling from Florida. He wishes Eddie happy birthday and then talks about his grandson and his new apartment on the beach.

He is eighty-two. A Tuesday. He slides into the front seat of a taxi at the park entrance, pulling his cane in behind him.

"Most people like to sit in the back," the driver says.

"You mind?" Eddie asks.

"No, I don't mind," the driver says.

Eddie looks straight ahead. It feels more like driving this way, and he hasn't driven since they refused him a license two years ago.

The taxi takes him to the cemetery. He visits his mother's and Joe's graves; he stands by his father's grave for less time. As usual, he saves his wife's for last. He leans on his cane, and thinks about many things. Candy from the boardwalk, his favorite candy. He thinks it would pull his teeth out now, but he would eat it anyway, if he could eat it with her.

♦

THE LAST LESSON

The little girl appeared to be from an Asian country, maybe five or six years old, with beautiful light brown skin, dark black hair, a small flat nose, a joyful smile, and dark, happy eyes. She smiled and waved her hands excitedly until Eddie came one step closer and she introduced herself.

"Tala," she said, offering her name, placing her hands on her chest.

"Tala," Eddie repeated.

She smiled and began her game. She pointed to her blouse. "*Baro*," she said.

"*Baro*," Eddie repeated.

"*Saya*," she said as she touched her red skirt.

"*Saya*."

Then she pointed at her shoes: "*bakya*"—then the seashells at her feet: "*capiz*"—then a small piece of carpet on the ground in front of her: "*banig*."

"Sit, please," she said to Eddie. They both sat on the carpet. The children continued to play in the river and paid no attention to them. Eddie watched one boy rub a stone over the body of another, down his back, under his arms.

"Washing," the girl said. "Like our *inas* used to do."

"*Inas?*" Eddie said.

She studied Eddie's face. "Mommies," she said.

She pointed to Eddie's shirt pocket. He looked down. Balloons.

"These?" he said. He pulled one out, blew it up, and began to twist it, as he had done on his days at Ruby Park. The little girl watched him closely. His hands shook. "See? It's a ..." he finished the last twist "... dog."

She took it and smiled—a smile Eddie had seen a thousand times on children at Ruby Park.

"You like that?" he said.

"You burn me," she said.

Eddie's jaw felt tight. "What did you say?"

"You burn me. You make fire. My *ina* say to wait inside the *nipa*. My *ina* say to hide."

Eddie spoke quietly. His words were slow and cautious.

"What ... were you hiding *from*, little girl?"

She placed her balloon dog in the water.

"*Sundalong*," she said.

"*Sundalong?*"

She looked up. "Soldier," she said in her quiet, serious voice.

Eddie felt the word like a knife. Pictures flashed through his head. Soldiers. Explosion. Morton, Smitty. The Captain. The flame-throwers.

"Tala ..." he whispered. "Why are you here in heaven? Were you in the Philippines? Were you the shadow I saw in that hut?"

"The *nipa*. The hut. *Ina* say be safe there. Wait for her. Be safe. Then big noise. Big fire. You burn me. Not safe."

Eddie buried his face in his hands. The darkness that had followed him all those years was lifting at last. Now he saw real flesh and blood, this child, this beautiful child—he had killed her, burned her to death. He had deserved every bad dream he'd ever had. He *had* seen something! That shadow in the flame! Death by his hand! *By his own hand!* Tears covered his fingers and his soul seemed to fall into a deep hole.

He screamed, and then a cry rose within him in a voice he had never heard before. His cries were so loud that the air of heaven shook. Then he began to pray: "I killed you, I KILLED YOU. Forgive me. FORGIVE ME, OH, GOD, what have I done? WHAT HAVE I DONE?"

He cried and cried, until his tears made him shake. He was kneeling on the carpet while the little girl played calmly with her balloon animal beside the river.

When he was quiet again, Eddie felt a light touch on his shoulder. He looked up and saw Tala holding a stone.

"You wash me," she said. She stepped into the river and turned her back to Eddie. Then she pulled her blouse over her head.

Eddie was shocked. Now her skin was terribly burned. Her body and narrow shoulders were black and covered with scabs. When she turned around, her beautiful, innocent face was gone. She was burned beyond recognition. Her lips hung down. Only one eye was open. Most of her hair was gone, and her head was covered with more scabs and red burns.

"You wash me," she said again, holding out the stone.

Eddie limped to the river. He took the stone. His fingers shook.

"I don't know how ..." he whispered. "I didn't have any children ..."

She raised her burned hand and Eddie took it gently and slowly rubbed the stone along her arm, until the scabs began to fall away. He rubbed harder and the burned flesh fell and the healthy flesh re-appeared. He rubbed her thin back and tiny shoulders, and finally her cheeks and her forehead and the skin behind her ears and around her eyes and mouth. He rubbed her head and watched her healthy, thick hair grow out of the roots.

She was a beautiful child again. When she opened her eyes, she whispered, "I am five."

Eddie put the stone on the sand. "Five? Five years old?"

She shook her head no. She held up five fingers. Then she pushed them against Eddie's chest: *Your* five. *Your fifth.*

A tear rolled down Eddie's cheek. Tala studied it in the way a child studies an insect in the grass. Then she spoke to the space between them.

"Why sad?" she said.

"Why am I sad?" he whispered. "Here?"

She pointed down, toward Earth. "There."

Eddie stopped crying. His chest felt empty. He tried to explain himself to this child. He said what he always said, to Marguerite, to Ruby, to the Captain, to the Blue Man, and, more than anyone, to himself.

"I was sad because I didn't do anything with my life. I was nothing. I didn't do anything important. I was lost. I felt like I wasn't supposed to be there."

Tala picked up her balloon dog.

"*Supposed* to be there," she said.

"Where? At Ruby Park?"

"Yes," she said.

"Fixing rides? That was the meaning of my whole life?" He took a deep breath. "Why?"

She smiled at him. Wasn't it obvious?

"Children," she said. "You keep them safe. Is where you were supposed to be." She touched his shirt pocket with a laugh and added two words: "Eddie Main-ten-ance."

♦

Eddie sat in the rushing water. The stones of his stories were all around him now, beneath the surface, one touching another. He had met his five people in heaven. What would happen next?

83

"Tala?" he whispered. She looked up. "The little girl at the park? Do you know about her?"

"Yes," Tala answered, staring at her hands.

"Did I save her? Did I pull her out of the way?"

"No pull."

Eddie's head dropped to his chest. So there it was. The end of his story.

"Push," Tala said.

Eddie looked up. "Push?"

"Push her legs. No pull. You push. Big thing fall. You keep her safe."

Eddie shut his eyes and tried to remember. "But I felt her hands," he said. "It's the only thing I remember clearly. I'm *sure* I didn't push her. I felt her *hands*."

Tala smiled and then placed her small fingers in Eddie's adult hands. He understood immediately. They had been there before. "Not *her* hands," she said. "Those were *my* hands. I bring you to heaven. Keep you safe."

♦

Now the river rose quickly, coming up higher than Eddie's shoulders. The noise of the children disappeared above him, and he was swept away by the river. Tala still held his hands, and pulled him gently through shadow and light, through every color he had seen in heaven, and he realized that all these colors were the emotions of his life. He felt all of his pain and worry and regret wash away. Tala pulled him through the enormous waves of a great gray ocean, and he rose up into wonderfully bright light, into an unimaginable scene:

There was an amusement park filled with thousands of people, men and women, fathers and mothers and children. Children from the past and the present, children who had not yet been born, side by side, hand in hand, filling the boardwalk and the rides and the wooden platforms, sitting on each other's shoulders. They were there, or would be there, because of the simple, everyday things Eddie had done in his life, the accidents he had prevented, the rides he had kept safe. And although their lips did not move, Eddie heard their voices, more voices than he thought was possible, and a peace came over him that he had never known before. He was free of Tala's hands now, and he floated up above the sand and above the boardwalk, above the tents, toward the top of the big, white Ferris wheel, where one of the cars, moving gently, held a woman in a yellow dress. It was his wife, Marguerite, waiting with her arms held out to him. He reached for her and he saw her smile, and the voices below him joined together in a single word from God:

Home.

Afterword

Ruby Park opened again three days after the accident. The story of Eddie's death was in the newspapers for a week, and then other stories about other deaths took its place.

The ride called Freddy's Free Fall was closed for the season, but the next year it reopened with a new name, Devil's Drop. Teenagers saw it as proof of their courage; it attracted many customers, and the owners were pleased.

Eddie's apartment, the one he had grown up in, was rented to someone new, who moved things around and blocked the view of the old carousel. Dominguez, who had agreed to take Eddie's job, put the few things that Eddie had owned in a box in the maintenance shop, beside the old papers about the park, including photos of the original entrance.

Nicky, the young man whose key had cut the cable in

Freddy's Free Fall, returned often to Ruby Park, where he liked to tell his friends that his great-grandmother was the woman for whom it was named.

Seasons came and seasons went. And when school ended for the summer and the days grew long, the crowds returned to the amusement park by the great gray ocean—not as large as those at the theme parks, but large enough. In summer, the seashore calls with a song of the waves, and people want to go on rides, drink sweet iced drinks, and eat candy as they walk along the boardwalk.

Lines formed at Ruby Park—and a line formed somewhere else: Five people, waiting, in five chosen memories, for a little girl named Amy or Annie to grow and to love and to age and to die, and to finally have her questions answered—why she lived and what she lived for. And in that line now was an old man with white hair, carrying a cane and wearing a Ruby Park uniform. He was waiting in the Stardust Room to share his part of the secret of heaven: that each affects the other and the other affects the next, and the world is full of stories, but the stories are all one.

ACTIVITIES

Chapter 1

Before you read

1 Explain why you think people enjoy amusement parks. Do *you*? Describe your favorite ride.

2 Look at the Word List at the back of the book. Find the names of four popular rides at an amusement park.

3 Work with a partner. Look at the Word List again. Then discuss examples of:

   a places that you can decorate with *balloons*, and reasons for using them

   b machines that have a *cable*

   c reasons for using a *candle*

   d ways to mark a grave in a *cemetery*

   e activities for which you should wear a *helmet*

   f reasons for doing *maintenance* on your house

   g causes of walking with a *limp*

   h ways to earn a gold *medal*

   i ways in which a child can suffer *neglect*

   j reasons for making a *sacrifice*

4 Describe your idea of heaven. Where do your ideas come from? From your religion? From your imagination? From movies, books, or paintings?

While you read

5 Mark these sentences **T** (true) or **F** (false). Then compare your answers with another student's, and explain them with information from the story.

   a Ruby Park is one of the most modern amusement parks in the country.   .....

   b Eddie's face, body, and clothes show people that he is a working man.   .....

   c Teenagers who come to Ruby Park always respect Eddie and follow the rules.   .....

d	Dominguez is Eddie's boss.	.....
e	Eddie's love for Marguerite begins on the night he meets her and lasts all his life.	.....
f	Amy (or Annie) always comes to Ruby Park with her grandparents.	.....
g	Eddie entertains children at the park by making balloon animals for them.	.....
h	Nicky's lost car key causes the accident that kills Eddie.	.....
i	Only two of the passengers escape from Freddy's Free Fall before it crashes to the ground.	.....
j	The last thing Eddie sees before he dies is the little girl with her balloon rabbit.	.....

After you read

6 Find the places in the story where the writer mentions how many minutes Eddie has to live. What is happening at each of these times? How does this countdown to Eddie's death affect your understanding of the story?

7 Work in pairs. Eddie's body has been taken away in an ambulance. Act out the conversation between the fat woman who first notices the problem with Freddy's Free Fall and a newspaper reporter who has just arrived at the scene of the accident.

Chapter 2

Before you read

8 Eddie dies because he tries to save a little girl's life. What do you think happens to her?

9 Look at the title of Chapter 2. List the kinds of people that you expect Eddie to meet in heaven.

While you read

10 Mark each of Eddie's actions according to where it happens: **E** (only on Earth), **H** (only in heaven), **B** (both on Earth and in heaven).

| **a** | floats from place to place | ..... |

b has no physical pain ·····

c feels sadness, worry, and regret ·····

d sits in a big teacup ride ·····

e needs to use a cane ·····

f can't shout or speak ·····

g looks old in his Ruby Park uniform ·····

h has white hair and runs and jumps ·····

i feels sorry for the Odd Citizens ·····

j sees the Blue Man ·····

11 Circle the right information about the Blue Man.

   a He was born in *Poland / the United States*.

   b His family was *rich / poor*.

   c As a child, he was *relaxed and happy / nervous and afraid*.

   d He had a *cruel / kind* father.

   e His skin turned blue because of *blueberries / silver nitrate*.

   f His blue skin *scared / charmed* people at the factory.

   g His job at Ruby Park *saved / ruined* him.

   h He *never / sometimes* played cards with Eddie's father.

   i He was a *confident / nervous* driver.

   j He died *alone / with his family around him*.

   k After his meeting with Eddie in heaven, his skin looks *worn out / beautiful*.

After you read

   12 Work with a partner. Discuss Eddie's birthdays.

   a How does Eddie's father feel on the day his son is born?

   b Why is Eddie happy on his seventh birthday?

   c Why is the funeral on Eddie's eighth birthday important to his life in heaven?

   d Why is Eddie's birthday during the war both bitter and sweet?

   e Why does the author use present-tense verbs in the birthday sections?

Chapter 3

Before you read

   13 How do you expect Eddie's body to feel when he meets

his second person in heaven? What do you base your
expectations on?

14 Do you think the next person Eddie meets in heaven will be
someone that he hardly knew on Earth, like the Blue Man,
or someone he knew well? Who might it be?

While you read

15 Write the name of the person who has these thoughts.

a "Eddie is too dumb to go to college." ....
....

b "In war, you must not feel any pity for your enemy." ....
....

c "Prisoners-of-war must not become friendly with their
guards." ....

d "I need a doctor. I can't go back into that mine." ....
....

e "The sick guy is useless to us. Better dead." ....
....

f "I wish I could learn to juggle with these rocks." ....
....

g "I hope Rabozzo knows what we did to the Crazies." ....
....

h "I'll be waiting for Eddie when the war ends." ....
....

i "Our flame-throwers will show them who the boss is." ....
....

j "My army background guided my actions." ....
....

After you read

16 After the war, Eddie has terrible dreams. Based on this
chapter, describe what you think the content of these dreams
could be. You can draw pictures, too, if you like.

Chapter 4

Before you read

17 Discuss the qualities a good parent should have. Are these

different for fathers and mothers? Does each of the two parents have a different role in their children's lives?

While you read

18 In which order do we read these sections in Chapter 4? Write the numbers 1—10.

    a Eddie's father prefers cards and drink to the responsibilities of being a good father. .....

    b Ruby Park is destroyed by fire. .....

    c Preparations are made for Eddie's funeral. .....

    d Eddie is surprised by the sight of his father sitting in an old-fashioned café. .....

    e Eddie learns the truth about his father's illness and death. .....

    f Eddie's father argues with him and then stops speaking to him. .....

    g Eddie returns to the old café in the snow to mend his relationship with his father. .....

    h Eddie faces his birthday after a night of bad dreams. .....

    i Eddie spends a birthday in an army hospital. .....

    j Ruby tells the story of her life and the building of Ruby Park. .....

After you read

19 Make two lists. In the first, give specific examples of ways in which Eddie's father damages him. In the second, give examples of actions which show that Eddie's father is not a totally bad person.

20 Work with a partner. Discuss the reasons why both Ruby and Eddie regret that Ruby Park ever existed. What kind of life would have been possible for each of them without Ruby Park?

Chapter 5

Before you read

21 What happens at a traditional wedding celebration in your country? Describe the most interesting wedding you have been to.

22 Marguerite's phrase, *"Per l'amaro e il dolce,"* is similar to a
phrase in many traditional wedding ceremonies in which the
couple promise to stay together, "for better, for worse, for
richer, for poorer, in sickness and in health."

   a Find three bitter experiences that Eddie and Marguerite
     have in their life together.

     1 ....

     2 ....

     3 ....

   b Find three sweet things about their life together.

     1 ....

     2 ....

     3 ....

   c Write down three sweet things about their meeting
     in heaven.

     1 ....

     2 ....

     3 ....

After you read

23 Work with a partner. Discuss why these are important to the
story of Eddie and Marguerite.

   a candy

   b Joe's success

   c Sammy Hong's

   d Jersey Finch

   e an empty alcohol bottle

   f adoption

   g their special song

   h the distant Ferris wheel

Chapter 6

Before you read

24 What question does Eddie desperately want to find the
answer to when he arrives in heaven? Has he found the
answer yet?

25 Write three words or phrases to describe these children.

    a The thousands of children playing in the river

        1 ....

        2 ....

        3 ....

    b Tala, before Eddie learns what happened to her

        1 ....

        2 ....

        3 ....

    c Tala, after Eddie learns what he did

        1 ....

        2 ....

        3 ....

26 In heaven, Eddie sees an amusement park.

    a What adjective best describes the park?

    ....

    b What noun describes Eddie's feelings as he looks at it?

    ....

27 What is Eddie waiting for now? Why?

    He is waiting for .... ,

    so ....

28 Match the people Eddie meets in heaven with the lessons they teach him.

    a the Blue Man   **1)** Life has to end, but love doesn't.

    b the Captain   **2)** It is important to be loyal and to forgive.

    c Ruby   **3)** All lives are connected. Birth and death are part of a whole.

    d Marguerite   **4)** Eddie was, in his lifetime, where he was supposed to be.

    e Tala   **5)** Sacrifices are something to work toward. Promises should be kept.

29 Which lesson do you consider the most important one to remember in your life?

Afterword

Before you read

30 While Eddie is in heaven, what do you think is happening at Ruby Park?

While you read

31 In your own words, what do we learn about:

a Freddy's Free Fall?

....

b Eddie's apartment?

....

c Dominguez?

....

d Nicky?

....

After you read

32 Act out this conversation

Student A: You are visiting your friend and have come to Ruby Park. You want to go on the ride called Devil's Drop. Persuade your friend to go with you.

Student B: You know the history of the ride and are very nervous about trying it. Explain to your friend why you don't want to go on it.

Writing

33 You are a newspaper reporter. Write a report on the fire at the original Ruby Park. Emile has been injured and the whole place has burned down.

34 Eddie and Marguerite are in love before Eddie goes to war. Write a list of the goals that they hope to achieve in their life together after the war.

35 Write a conversation between Eddie and Dominguez. Begin with Dominguez's question: "What did you do in World War II, Eddie?"

36 Write what Eddie's father wants to say to his wife and to Eddie on the night he dies, as he looks out his hospital window.

37 Imagine that you are Mickey Shea. Write a letter to Eddie's mother after her husband dies. Try to explain the reasons for your terrible behavior, apologize, and promise to act differently in the future.

38 Write a short speech for Dominguez to give at Eddie's funeral service *or* for Eddie to give at his wife's funeral service.

39 Imagine that Dominguez does not want Eddie's job as Head of Maintenance at Ruby Park. Think about the experience and skills that are needed for the job. Write an advertisement for the job to put in the local newspaper.

40 Write a conversation between one of these pairs of people, on this particular occasion:

   a Eddie and his mother, when his father stops speaking to Eddie.

   b Eddie and Marguerite, after Marguerite's brain tumor is discovered.

   c Amy/Annie and Eddie, when they meet in heaven.

41 The Blue Man says, "This step of heaven has finished for me." Write a description of a possible next step in heaven for one of the five people that Eddie meets there.

42 You are a magazine writer and are going to interview the author of this book, Mitch Albom. Write a list of questions that you want to ask him.

WORD LIST

adopt (v) to make someone else's child legally your son or daughter

arcade (n) a place where people put coins in machines and play games

balloon (n) a small, colored rubber bag that is filled with air to use as a toy or decoration

bumper cars (n pl) a ride at an amusement park in which people drive small cars and safely crash into other small cars

cable (n) a thick, strong metal rope

candle (n) a stick of wax that you burn to produce light

cane (n) a long, thin stick used to help you walk

carousel (n) a machine with wooden horses that turns around and around and that people ride on for fun

cemetery (n) a place where dead people are buried

dog tag (n) a metal label worn on a chain around the neck by men and women in the army. It gives information about the wearer.

Ferris wheel (n) an amusement park ride consisting of a large upright turning wheel and seats for passengers

fireworks (n pl) small objects that, when lighted, explode or burn with bright colors. Fireworks are used for special celebrations.

freak (n) someone who is considered very strange because of the way he or she looks, behaves, or thinks

helmet (n) a hard hat that covers and protects your head

juggle (v) to keep a number of objects moving through the air by throwing and catching them very quickly

limp (n/v) the way someone walks, with difficulty, when one leg is hurt

maintain (v) to keep something, especially a machine or a building, in good condition. The work that is necessary for this is **maintenance**.

medal (n) a round, flat piece of metal given as a prize to someone who has been very brave, or has won a sports competition